Paul Cree is a poet, storyteller, rap
has been performing regularly ar
events such as Ronnie Scott's, T
Centre, Roundhouse, Camden P
Wilderness, Bestival and the Edi
having his work showcased on BBC 1Xtra. He has written and performed 2 solo shows; *A Tale From The Bedsit* (2013) and *The C/D Borderline* (2016) as well as co-writing and performing in the critically acclaimed *No Milk For The Foxes* (2015). He has an EP of stories entitled *The 90 Sick E.P* produced by Elian Gray. When not engaging with any of the above, Paul works regularly with young people and enjoys drinking mugs of tea whilst staring aimlessly out of the window, consuming pints of lager with his mates and following football.

'Maria' was originally performed in the theatre show *A Tale from the Bedsit*, and 'Creatine' and 'HMS Geezer' in *The C/D Borderline.*

'The 21.00 To Nowhere' and 'She Says' originally featured in *Rhyming Thunder – the Alternative Book of Young Poets* (Burning Eye, 2012).

The Suburban

Paul Cree

Burning Eye

BurningEyeBooks
Never Knowingly
Mainstream

This edition published by Burning Eye Books 2018

www.burningeye.co.uk

@burningeyebooks

Burning Eye Books
15 West Hill, Portishead, BS20 6LG

ISBN 978-1-911570-30-1

The Suburban

"Paul's that guy. He tells it how it is. And it's like, 'Rah. That's just how it is.' He writes as well as he drinks: well."

Conrad Murray, artist

"Unpretentious, funny, honest, insightful: Paul Cree's performances – and now, his stories and poems on the page – offer snapshots of unheralded outer-London life, of Streets of Rage, the Sun and sick trainers, of BBQ Hula Hoops and a big heart. His is a unique voice, and I love it."

Brian Logan, journalist and artistic director of Camden People's Theatre

To Mum and Dad, thank you for everything.

Thank you and rest in peace to Bill Mitchell and Nicola Thorold, two giants who showed belief in me.

CONTENTS

Pre-Introduction 13
Proper Introduction 14
Prologue 17

Part 1: Underneath the Flight Path

Bright Lights in the Shadow 20
Games of Rage 21
Highland Blues 22
Fair and Square 24
The Colour Orange 25
HMS Geezer 30
Grass Grazer 37
Creatine 39
Lost Days Lost 44
No Frills 46
Jungle Warfare 48
The Irony of It All 52
Coke Can 54
Whoever Said It Was Easy 56

Part 2: Belly Flop

London Calling 62
The 21.00 to Nowhere 64
Montage 66
Maria 68
A Pale Shade of White 73
Small Talk 74
The 12 78
She Says 79
Giftwrapped 80

Embankment 82
Plastics 83
Catching Confetti 84
Priorities 85
Northern Line 87
Your Nails 88
Turbo Breeze 89
Infant 92
All This About Broken Hearts 94
The 159 95
Cement Legs 96

Part 3:When It All Stopped Making Sense

Morden Sunrise 100
Crows 101
Rhythm 103
Stations of the Cross 105
The Atheist 107
Trap It 109
Two to Tango 111
One More 112
Blame It on the Tracking 114
Inferno 116
Epilogue: 118

PRE-INTRODUCTION

I'm not sure if someone like me is supposed to do an introduction for this book. Does that make me a bit of a bellend now that I have? I think if you do have one, someone else is supposed to do it, right? But even then, introductions, that's for, like, proper writers, yeah? The ones that sell their books in supermarkets, with the embossed front covers (I love the feel of those!). Oh well, this book may well be my one crack at all this, so I'm making the most of it, mate. You can always skip on, or jog on; up to you. I just thought it would be good to try and explain a few things before you get stuck in.

Seriously, though, if you are reading this, or if you are one of the numerous good-hearted people who have helped me out over the years with gigs, advice, opportunities, money or just simple pick-me-ups, or if you've seen me perform and spoken to me after a show, thank you. I sincerely hope you enjoy this. I've had a great time.

PROPER INTRODUCTION

(written by me, so probably not proper, then?)

When I think about it, you know, all this writing and performing stuff, it makes me wonder whether all the best things in life really are just totally irrational and inexplicable. I genuinely love doing this: writing stuff – stories, poems, raps, scripts, whatever – and then getting up and performing it. There's not a lot else I want to do with my life (this or driving the Volk's railway up and down Brighton Marina; that would be sick). However, thinking about a thing, or things, then writing words down about those things and then finally speaking those things out loud are all things, as separate things, that I've always struggled with. It doesn't make any sense to me that I've wound up doing this.

Firstly, my spelling is so bad that often spellcheck will produce a list of words that are nowhere near what I'm trying to spell, or produce no words at all, as if it's given up and gone, 'Nah, mate, don't even bother.' Regarding my handwriting, one of my brothers often jokes that it looks like a mass murderer's, whatever that looks like (though I've managed to improve it by working as a teaching assistant at a primary school; I can write cursive now!). Putting this book together put the tremors up me. There's ten years' worth of stuff here. When I first started writing these poems, I couldn't even be arsed to turn the caps lock off and would just write in block capitals for no reason. If there was a spellcheck equivalent of a Geiger counter, going through this book would probably smash the glass, and thank God the manuscript was in digital form and not handwritten; I'd imagine it would be like trying to read the writing of a mass murderer, whatever that looks like.

From as far back as I remember, I've had people making remarks about how I speak, or how I sound when I speak, and often it can be quite insulting. I became very self-conscious about it as a teen, being all too aware that I sound like I've got peanuts shoved up my nose. 'Speak properly' is something that was bleated at me quite a lot as a nipper, or 'you sound like you're stoned' as I got older, as well as a bunch of other more offensive comments. What some of these people may not have understood, or cared about, is that I find speaking quite difficult. It takes a lot of effort for me to fully form words in my mouth and often I can't even get them out; it's like they get log-jammed somewhere between my throat and lips and what comes out is some sort of low-frequency word pulp that barely constitutes a sentence. The number of job interviews, dates, meetings etc. that I've completely blown just from opening my mouth. At some point, I think I figured I'd never be able to 'speak properly' and just carried on as I was, in fact eventually going on to own that imperfection. What's nuts to me is, despite how embarrassed I felt about it (and still do), when I did get up to rap lyrics into a microphone or read my little poems, people listened! They listened, and they clapped and cheered (most of the time), and it still baffles me to this day. Maybe, just maybe, those imperfections make me stand out a bit? If that's the case, then it's karma, mate. Makes me chuckle sometimes, thinking back to all the shit I took for it (and still get, by the way) and all the amazing things I've been able to gain from it since, mugs.

The final component in all of this is thinking: daydreaming, I suppose. By the time I commit something to paper, or the computer, chances are it's swum around my head for a number of hours, days, weeks, months, years before even seeing the light of day; without daydreaming, there would be nothing to write. I can spend a long time in my own head. It's not healthy, but occasionally stuff like the material in this book comes out.

I genuinely used to think there was something wrong with me, like my brain was wired up incorrectly. It took me years to realise that I just have a bit of an overactive imagination, and that's OK, so long as I put it to good use. Daydreaming was not something that was ever encouraged, and it often got me in trouble, not paying attention in class, church and most jobs I've ever had, where I've made costly mistakes on the spreadsheets, soldered the wrong component, sorted the letters into the wrong postcode, cleaned the wrong room etc. There are times when I really wish I could engage with the present more, like staring at GCSE exam papers with no clue as to what I'm looking at and no recollection of ever even studying it. Performing on stage is one of the few times when I do feel present.

What's worse is when my imagination goes into silly mode and I start thinking about situations that make me laugh, because, naturally, I start laughing, and this can get me in trouble. It happens a lot, often at the most inappropriate times. I've been sat in important meetings when all of a sudden I've started thinking about all of the world's leading finance, tech, petroleum and entertainment industries relocating to Morden and dining in the revolving restaurant at the top of the Civic Centre, or at Fish and Kebabs, over the road, then taking their seats in the grandstand, in front of Lidl, to watch the F1 racers ripping down Martin Way. 'So, Paul, what do you think you can bring to this project?' 'Er...'

When I get asked why I do what I do and I think about all of the above, it doesn't make any sense to me, as all those things have caused me no end of grief over the years. All I can say is that I just have this desire to do it, to write and perform. It excites me. It's often frustrating and hard to control that excitement, but it's never gone away; it's still there and it's the driving force behind all of this. What's great is that I really enjoy it, I love it, and somehow, when all of those above things combine, it just works, mate. It doesn't make any sense to me, but then, none of the best things do, do they?

A big thank you to Kyra Hall-Gelly for helping me shape this thing, Harriet Evans for the mammoth task of editing, Natalie Clay for the cover design, and Bridget and Clive at Burning Eye for putting it all out.

Paul Cree
September 2017

PROLOGUE

Sometimes I think up the greatest ideas,
sometimes I think myself out of the greatest ideas,
sometimes I think that I think too much about not
thinking, wishing that the vacancy of space created
by thoughtlessness will give me some peace and clarity, a
perfect climate for thinking; now
there's a thought.

PART 1:

UNDERNEATH THE FLIGHT PATH

BRIGHT LIGHTS IN THE SHADOW

The immortal orange glow swallows stars.
Nearby farms sit underneath the flight
path surrounded by motorway.
Paradoxes of tranquillity tucked behind
B-roads, where rows of three and four-bed detached
houses fetch value like the well-trained thoroughbred
dogs seen on the alleyways and bridleways, fetching
castaway branches, to the arms of masters who make
money in the city and home in the shadow, where the
orange glow of the airport provides employment for those
unable to brave the cattle of the packed commuter
trains to the trades of the city.

Baggage handlers boss the pubs and
commandeer the pool tables. Stewards
hold court on the dance floors of bars
that try hard to attain the status of their bigger
city cousins, yet still charge the same prices. Kids
compete with eager fists to be the biggest fish in
the garden pond, unaware there is a whole world
out there, beyond the orange glow and the shadow
that hangs from the city, distinguishing
province from capital.

GAMES OF RAGE

We're playing Streets of Rage, me and Will, fighting the baddies together. He's older, gets the best control pad, I get the clunky third-party one with the unresponsive buttons. Will's good at computer games. Dedicated. I'm alright. Not as bothered as him. I lack the focus. Get into it for a few minutes, then I just drift. Mainly when it gets a bit difficult. Funny, that; sounds a bit like school.

We're on level four. So far, I've resisted bashing him. You can do that on this game, you can bash your partner. Kills off the character, though, leaving the other to fight the baddies alone. Two heads and all that. I'm being good. It's really hard, though, really hard.

In the long term, I know there's far more satisfaction to be had completing the game together. Yet the short term is so much more tempting. Abandon the baddies and just batter him with the big metal pole. Right now it's so much more appealing than the boss we're about to face. That's gonna be... hard.

Last time I did it, he said he'd beat me up for real. My head's hurting; takes a lot of concentrating, this. Will is sat in a weird crouch position, like a squirrel on its hind legs protecting a nut, two hands on the controller, eyes locked on the screen, as if the sheer intensity of his stare is causing the occasional fuzz from the half-hanging-out SCART lead.

I've just picked up the big metal pole. My character is walking towards his character. Am I doing this? Yes. I'm doing this, bashing him with the big metal pole. Man down. He fades on screen and disappears. That sound rings out through the shitty side-speakers in the telly to signal digital death. Will's now bashing me for real. Game over. I gave in.

HIGHLAND BLUES

My dad's fuse was short. My youth was spent carelessly walking on eggshells, fearing the much bigger figure of my father's authority, casting a shadow over parts of my childhood. I knew where the line was, often crossing it to my regret, learning first-hand what it feels like to have both bum-cheeks resembling a blushing boy about to embark on a first kiss. Yet there were no lips to cushion the connection, just the hard, cold sole of a leather slipper, followed by tearful apologies and half-hearted promises of never doing it again, whatever it was I'd done.

My status as a child frustrated me, exemplified by the times my father would place a man-sized hand on top of my head, palm spread, arm outstretched, letting me swing hopelessly with left and right, punching nothing but the air between him and my young body frame. He was the man. I was the boy lacking reach.

Back then I understood little of my parents' plight. Sacrifices they'd made so my siblings and I could live in a heated house. Dad worked a job he really didn't like, often arriving home tired, skint and stressed, to be greeted by stories of disobedient children. It's no surprise we'd sometimes be made to sit and eat dinner in silence, quietly fearing he might flip.

Saturday afternoons, the front room at home was a no-go zone. It was Dad's time. He'd listen to the blues programme on Radio 2. I didn't understand much, but I understood this was my father's one moment of solitude and I never questioned it, only empathised. And it was upon these radio wavelengths we retrospectively bonded. Occasionally I'd be invited in, on the condition I sat in silence and just listened. I felt privileged to be admitted; it gave me an insight into an adult's life I wanted but rarely glimpsed.

I'd sit on the small sofa opposite Dad, sat in his chair, and tap my feet in time with his, synced to the warmth of Muddy Waters, radiating out of the radio and into skin pores, soothing wounds from stressful weeks. We listened. We tapped. Sat in silence. Those were some of the best conversations we ever had.

My dad was the son of a Glaswegian, who in turn came from a place they call the gateway to the highlands. Through both sets of grandparents, I'm Irish on one side, Scots on the other. Raised in England with English-born parents, I'm practically Anglicised, yet I recognise personality traits which I don't associate with the English. I'm told of a quiet melancholy that resides deep in some Scotsmen, rarely seeing the light of the day, expressed only in rare moments of cohesion. I was always taught to hold emotion; expression was a concept belonging to the privileged. Consequently, I find emotion a little bit difficult to deal with; it's akin to driving a car when you've never driven nor held the desire to drive, preferring instead to be left alone to walk, and that's when that deep-rooted, inherited melancholy talks of highland blues.

If I'm listening to music, or I'm watching Match of the Day, unless you're willing to sit with me in silence then leave me be, or a wee plastic Scotsman in a gift shop kilt and bonny hat might just snap and jump out of his tree.

If it's possible to strengthen a bond via the nerve endings of memory, then I just did. Muddy Waters is king of the blues, Scotland is the land of the brave and when I hear 'Fields of Athenry' play, and no one's looking, sometimes my eyes well up.

FAIR AND SQUARE

Sports day at middle school she beat
me in the penalty contest. The
underdog mauling the
favourite.

Her clean three strikes to my
two and one complete miskick.

She held her nerve as she
does today like a grenade pin
gripped by teeth. I
lost mine, along
with my pride.

Her face held the firmest of
foundations, cradling a
cauldron of concentration and
determination as she tucked each
shot in the bottom corner of the net
against what was then one of the
best keepers in the school.

She said she meant it.
I said it was a fluke.
It didn't matter.
Her face that day
said it all.

She wanted it more than me.

That day, in front of
all my mates, my
little sister won the
sports day penalty
contest, fair
and square.

THE COLOUR ORANGE

He's on telly again. The man with the permanent suntan, funny accent, white teeth and shiny face. Often seen on TV bending spoons with his mind, like some sort of bastard child of Magneto and the Tubular Bells guy, dangerously mixed with that suspect cheery disposition that I only ever see in travelling Christian theatre companies, bouncing around my school stage, singing it in the valleys and shouting from the mountain tops.

The spoon bender is now enticing me to touch a big orange spot on my screen. This strange man seems to be smeared all over television, like the Oxy 10 I apply badly to my face each morning before school, looking in the mirror too scared to pop spots and wondering who Adam is and why he's stuck an apple in my throat. Each time I swallow it looks like a satsuma's being slipped down the inside of a snake.

The man with the permanent suntan, funny accent, white teeth and shiny face is making yet another TV appearance, on the special edition of the Baddiel and Skinner Fantasy Football show, which I'm watching, sat in the living room, on the well-worn settee, on my own.

Apparently, if I touch this big orange spot, the man with the permanent suntan, funny accent, white teeth and shiny face will become like a SCART lead and channel all that positive energy from televisions around the nation towards the England football team. It's Euro 96; they're playing Scotland the very next day! My grandpa, from Dad's side, is from Scotland. My older brother supports Scotland, he doesn't support England, he supports the other team when England play, and that really gets on my nerves! There's a lot at stake for this game.

I sink down onto the floral-patterned badly faded settee like a fence, watching the screen, picking splinters from my spleen. I roll my eyes up to the lopsided white wooden shelf on the back wall, on which sits a small collection of my thirteenth birthday cards, which have now managed to last for three days. They all seem to have the same picture, of a hand-drawn school locker with loads of sports equipment spilling out. Stood next to the cards in a permanent place is a small statue of the Virgin Mary from Lourdes. It contains some holy water and two decorative plates, which stand upright like shields and have pictures of both Glasgow and Belfast. Belfast is where my grandad comes from, on Mum's side. Underneath the lopsided white wooden shelf is the TV: a fourteen-inch black Philips box which doesn't have a remote, and sometimes the buttons get stuck and don't work.

Like a top gun fighter pilot, target in sight, my eyes lock back on to the big orange spot on the screen. The man with the permanent suntan, funny accent, white teeth and shiny face is enticing me. Touch faith, that song says.

I'm not sure what to believe, but I'm willing to give it a go. Mum and Dad probably won't like it, as I'm sure it goes against the teachings of the church, but so far God hasn't answered any of my prayers about girls and I've only just got a Sega Mega Drive; it's 1996! My best friend Rich has already got rid of his and now has a Sega Saturn. And, as for my teeth, I must be at the back of the longest queue in NHS history because I haven't seen an orthodontist yet, my teeth still look like Stonehenge and Richard calls me goofy. I slowly rise, walk towards the telly and stick my sweaty little palm on the static of the glass. Right on the orange spot. I'm doing it for England. I want England to win.

It's the following day and I'm now at Richard's house. He's got a much bigger TV; it's massive. He also has Sky; the satellite dish is outside his bedroom on the wall and apparently, at nightime, for ten minutes, there's a secret channel where you get to see naked women! He also watches WWF. I have to make do with WCW on ITV. His parents actually like football and on Sunday they take him to games and watch him play, they don't go to church. He has barbecues in his garden, holidays to Florida and places in Spain where they have outdoor water parks that Richard reckons are way better than the Croydon Water Palace. My family sit round playing guitars and other weird instruments with strings and sing silly-sounding songs in Irish accents.

I rode my brand-new bike which I got for my birthday up to Richard's. I say new; it's second-hand, but it's my first ever mountain bike. It's got Shimano gears and Rhino horns. Richard's got two mountain bikes; he keeps one spare.

We're both lying on our bellies in his living room, eyes fixed on his massive TV, waiting for the two arch-enemies to commence battle. I'm nervous. I want England to win. I didn't want to watch the game at home, as I knew my older brother would be there, in his Celtic shirt and Scotland scarf, and my dad, who doesn't really like football but will still watch the big games without taking sides. When a player rolls around the floor pretending to be injured, he'll go 'achhh' just like my grandpa does. I needed to be amongst my own, I want England to win.

The first forty-five fly by with turbulence. At half time, it's nil-nil and it's tense. The commentator is telling us that Jamie Redknapp is coming on from the bench; his instructions are to keep hold of the ball in midfield so the full backs can get forward. Richard and I erupt when Gary Neville swings in a cross from the right flank which Alan Shearer heads into the net to put England one-nil up! Rolling round on the floor, Rich trying to put me in the headlock and punch me!

Minutes later, out of nowhere, Scotland suddenly get a penalty! Gary McAllister steps up and places the ball on the spot, an expert executioner if ever there was one. I'm nervous. As he takes the few paces just before he strikes, something very strange happens: the ball moves ever so slightly, and when he connects, he hits it hard but Seaman saves and we erupt all over again! It's still one-nil and I'm trying to put Richard in the headlock now, rolling round on the carpet!

Now, apparently, at this very moment, hovering above Wembley in a helicopter, holding one of Bobby Moore's England caps, is the man with the permanent suntan, funny accent, white teeth and shiny face! The one who told me to touch the orange spot! It must have been him that moved the ball! And when Jamie Redknapp plays a sweeping pass, flicked on by Darren Anderton into the path of an advancing Paul Gascoigne, who in two amazing moves deftly clips the ball over Colin Hendry's head and slams it into the back of the net, Richard and I explode and go running round his garden, shouting our heads off!

The game's finished now, England won! I'm getting on my bike and all I can think about is claiming those rare bragging rights when I get home, as I know my brother was watching it. I start riding, cars in the street are beeping, I can hear people singing everywhere, that Baddiel and Skinner song, 'Football's Coming Home'. Displayed all over the place is the white and red flag of St George, which until Euro 96 I'd not really seen before, but now it's on almost every house. It's a good day to be English.

I ride my brand-new-second-hand bike back home. I can't wait to see my brother's face! I put my bike in the shed and come in through the back door into the kitchen. I can hear my dad on the phone, probably to Grandpa. I hear a few 'achhh's, which more or less confirms my suspicions. Grandpa normally rings around this time on a Saturday, just before Mum and Dad go to church.

My brother is sat in the living room, still wearing his Celtic shirt and Scotland scarf, sunk so low into the settee I can barely see his body. He's watching the news. Gazza's goal is doing a loop-the-loop. I pause by the door. He looks dejected and I suddenly feel like I've said something to upset someone, except I haven't said anything yet. I feel bad, so I decide not to gloat. I try to make light of it, by telling him how I touched the orange spot on the telly the night before and that man with the permanent suntan, funny accent, white teeth and shiny face was hovering in a helicopter above Wembley and must have made Gary McAllister miss his penalty. My brother doesn't look at me; he stays slumped on the settee, looking at the telly, and mumbles some words about the orange spot, something about church and Mum and Dad. He then says something I don't really understand but I know it's bad, about Belfast, Grandpa, Grandad, marches and some people called loyalists.

I can hear my dad calling me from the hall to go and speak to Grandpa. I remind myself that my new bike has got Shimano gears and Rhino horns and that it was four miles to Richard's house, so that's eight miles in total that I rode today, and I tell myself that it's probably best that I don't mention the score.

HMS GEEZER

So me and my best mate Rich are standing at the front of the ship. This pretty big, decommissioned, ex-Royal Navy destroyer ship called HMS *Bristol*. There's probably some proper Navy name that I should be using instead of *front of the ship*, some silly name like *shaft* or something. There seems to be some wacky Navy name for everything in cadets. Most of which I can't ever remember. Even the toilets are called the heads. Heads? Who comes up with this shit? *Head* has come to mean something a lot different now that I'm fourteen. Mind you, Rich reckons he got a blow job once in the youth-wing toilets off of Gareth's cousin, so maybe that's where the name comes from? Though he's probably bullshitting.

Rich loves all this cadet stuff. I only joined because I could get into the football team; I can't get in at school. Right now, Rich is playing it cool, leaning on the edge of the boat, back to the water, one boot on the rails, taking it all in, enjoying it, smoking a Sovereign cigarette, but I swear he's not taking it down. I'm bent over, hanging *on* to the rails, shaking, looking down into the dark murky water of Portsmouth harbour, wishing that Triton or some other sea creature would burst up out of the blue and haul me down into a magic coral underworld, where I'm taken captive by some buff mermaids who sing mad ten-part harmonies and hold me in a giant sea shell, next to some weird undulating plants. Away from all this embarrassment and away from all the prying eyes burning holes in the back of this shitty, uncomfortable green uniform I've got on.

I just got asked out, by a girl! Who I thought yesterday, when I first stepped on this boat with all these other cadet kids, was about seventeen. Turns out she's also fourteen. And she's a senior cadet, whatever that means. Her name's Laura, she's got straight black hair in a bob and wears red lipstick, big brown eyes, smokes Embassy cigarettes, and Laura is fit. She was fit yesterday and she's even fitter now and she just asked *me* out, just now, in front of all the other cadet kids, on this big grey-arse knackered-looking Navy ship. Stuff like this doesn't really happen, ever!

Problem is, since getting on this boat, me and Rich have done well to assert ourselves as the geezers that we are and should be universally recognised as being. Letting these other cadet geeks know that we're no mugs, we're alright, but we've got a bit about us. Rich has even brought his Ralph Harrington jacket, and he's wearing it over his uniform. If I had a Ralph Harrington jacket, I'd be doing the same. Just today, me and Rich were schooling some of these cadet melts about how to spot a fake Ralph:

'If there ain't double stitching on the label, then someone's mugging you off!'

Letting these geeks know that we know about some real geezer stuff, like football, like even though Chelsea are from West London and Spurs are from North London, their firms hate each other and it always kicks off when those two play, always. And how if you twiddle with the flame adjuster, you can turn them cheap fluorescent cigarette lighters into mini-flamethrowers. Yeah, that's right, geezers. At school, we can't really pull it off, we get called Beavis and Butthead, but on this boat, we're like the flippin' Kray twins; most of these kids are pussies, into sailing and that. But unless I step up and get off with this girl, who I really fancy, I'm about to blow all that hard work out the water, quite literally!

Everyone is standing around, looking in my direction, waiting for me to say something. Each one of these thoughts and feelings whizzing around inside my brain is like those gold envelopes flapping about in the final challenge on *The Crystal Maze*, and I'm the dickhead in the booth, desperately trying to grab at them all and hide them from view.

'Er, I dunno, like… maybe, yeah,'

was what I came back with, whilst immediately turning round to lean on the rails, feeling like an instant bellend, that feeling that only girls seem to have access to, switching it on and manipulating it whenever they want, as if there's an invisible red button in my belly that only they have the codes to.

Rich asks me if I'm alright.

'Nah, mate, I feel ill. I must be, like, sea sick or something.'

'*Sea sick*? This boat don't move, mate, it hasn't moved in years, it stays in the harbour.'

'What? Yeah, I know, but it does move a little bit, like rocking back and forth and that, tides and that, doesn't it? I dunno, I just ain't feeling right.'

Rich looks at me and smiles.

'You're nervous, aren't ya?'

'No!'

'It's alright, bruv, it's your first time, yeah?'

'No, no, it ain't! You know it ain't! I told you, loads of times, that girl, Louise, from church, remember? I got on her loads of times, mate, Frenchies and everything, I even got feel-ups after confirmation class once.'

'Louise?'

Rich is grinning again, whilst pretending to rub a beard on his face. I don't know where this came from, but when someone says 'itchy beard' after you've just claimed something, and mimics rubbing their face, as if there's a beard there, it means they think you're lying. It's really, really annoying.

'Nah, mate, it's true!'

Rich takes another drag on his cigarette. He definitely doesn't take it down.

'Look... just say yes and get off with her, innit? She's fit.'

'Yeah, I know, but what if…'

'What? What if what?'

'What if I fuck it up?'

'You sure you've done this before?'

'Yeah, 'course! Louise!'

'Louise?'

'Yeah, Louise, from church.'

Rich looks back away from me, towards the waiting audience, and I think he's rubbing his chin again, one foot on the rail, facing right towards where Laura is standing, making me even more nervous! I want to see what he's doing, if he's communicating to them or not, but that would mean I'd have to turn around. I hear a little giggle behind me. Must be that Stef girl, who Rich hooked up with about ten minutes ago. She's mates with Laura, they're from the same cadet unit, ship, club or whatever the fuck it's called. I peer back down into the water below. I've given up on Triton and the mermaids rescuing me; my only hope now is that if I look hard enough, I'll see my reflection and all of a sudden, I'll have some deep poetic moment, like in *The Lion King*, when Simba sees Mufasa in the lake, and some life-changing epiphany will take place and I'll finally get the courage to stop being a melt and grow some balls!

I peer hard into the harbour water. I'm a bit too high up, the water is dark, can't really see much. There's an empty packet of BBQ Hula Hoops just floating aimlessly. If that's a sign, I don't really know what it means. I don't really like BBQ flavour, though I'll still eat it if there's nothing else in the multipack. The water is dark! Dark and pointless. Dark, pointless and wet. I swallow. Hoping there ain't any food stuck in my brace.

'Oi, Rich, is she looking?'

'Yep, she's looking, bruv, they all are. Hurry up, man, you're making yourself look like a pussy. Just count to ten, turn round, bowl over there and do the business, son. Enjoy it. I remember my first time like it was yesterday.'

'It's not my first… Louise… from church…'

I slowly turn around. I'm trying not to look at Laura, and instead stare at the air beyond her, like it's nothing, like I do this every day. They're all looking at me, must be like fifteen kids here. That Stef girl goes:

'So you gonna go out with her, yeah?'

'Yeah, yeah, alright,' I say.

'Tell her, then.'

I turn my face towards Laura. If she's nervous, she don't look it! She looks like this is nothing for her, like she does this every single day! I catch her big brown eyes and I quickly look away.

'Yeah,' I say.

She laughs. 'Yeah what?'

'Er, yeah. Yeah, I'll, like, go out with you, innit.'

'You gonna kiss me, then?'

I freeze. I spend so much time thinking about this sort of thing, whole lessons at school spent rehearsing these very moments in my head, over and over again, all the Lauras, Claires, Emmas, Hayleys, Rochelles, Geri Halliwells, all the Spice Girls and every other girl I've ever fancied, which is pretty much every girl I've ever met, yet it sounds and feels so weird saying it, saying *yes, I will go out with you*. And I start panicking, worrying that I have no clue what I'm doing or what I'm about to do, though my legs are moving, towards her, and suddenly we're doing it and her lips are on mine and moving. It's a bit wet, but we're connecting, it feels kinda good, bit messy, I'm not really moving my lips though, she is, shit, she's probably gonna think I don't know what I'm doing! Shit. I start moving mine and all of a sudden we start to sync, like those weird pulsating starfish stuck on the glass at Brighton sea-life centre, this is actually alright, this is amazing, this is magic or something, I'm getting into this, this is the best thing ever and *fuck, no*, I've got a boner! No, shit, she's gonna notice, everyone's gonna notice! I stick my bum out a bit and we carry on. Just hang in there, man, hang in there... we keep going, no one's said nothing, I just try and concentrate on how flipping good this is!

Eventually, we break the kiss. She slips out of my hold, but I pull her straight back into the embrace; can't let these mugs see that I've got a boner and plus I want another kiss! The other guys are cheering. I go in again, feel like I know a bit more about what I'm doing this time. Shit, this cadet crap ain't so bad after all. We kiss a bit longer this time and I have my eyes closed throughout. Wow.

When we eventually stop, most of the other kids have slid away, off to bed, or whatever stupid Navy name they give the bedrooms. I kiss her again, and again. I can't get enough. As we're coming off the deck, holding hands, her mate Stef hugs her and gives her £3.40 and two cigarettes.

'You win!'

she says to Laura, and they both share a joke about something. I don't ask what, I'm trying to be polite, we're an item now, she needs her own space. We say good night. I kiss her one last time by the kitchens, or whatever stupid Navy name they give it. Rich then appears, smelling of Lynx Africa and cigarettes. Putting his arm around me, he goes:

'Well done, son, you done it at last. Bit late to the party, bruv, but you made it.'

'Yeah, man, I think I really like her...'

'It's only a kiss, but I think we can let you in the big boys' club now, mate.'

'Yeah, yeah… the big boys' club… no, wait!'

'What?'

'I was already in the big boys' club… Louise, from… church.'

GRASS GRAZER

My body jolted, revolted at the sound of a floor-grappling guy engaged in a fight, being kicked full pelt in the face by a boot-wearing mate of his opponent. The crack from the contact of boot with face was a sound to induce stomach acid. Poor guy's nose exploded over his white school shirt and tie. Shriek shook leaves off the trees as he curled up in a ball, trying to protect his face, sports bag still attached to his back, only to be booted, a second time, in the same place, by the guy he was originally fighting with, who'd managed to wriggle away and get to his feet only after his boot-wearing mate threw in his foot uninvited. The surprise in the sound of the second shriek screamed of a man unfairly defeated.

Blood had dripped on to the grass verge where a group of us were stood, waiting for the bus, not knowing where to look. Couple of caring girls came running over with tissues for the wounded whilst the two face-kickers casually walked away.

The two boys brawling were in the year above me at school. One was a well-known rude boy, who carried way more attitude than weight, sporting blood on his expensive right Kicker shoe as he walked off, dressed in the latest puffa jacket, grass stains down his trousers, blond curtains flapping as he bopped to reveal a point-five undercut and two big gold hoops. The guy with the busted nose was quiet, didn't know his name, he was always playing football with the geeky kids, minding his own. The intervening boot-wearing third party, who pulled the unexpected chair from underneath the wrestling ring, was some mate of the rude boy who didn't go to my school and wasn't wearing a uniform.

From what I understood, the quiet guy was picked on, unprovoked, that teenage brand of primitive terror only rude boys administered. To that rude boy's surprise, though, quiet guy put up a resistance. Rude boy, flanked by his mate, didn't appear to like this, squared up to him, all pigeon chest, arms spread, head forward, physical threat, classic rude boy. And so the dust was upset and they tumbled, as me and a whole bunch of others rubbernecked with the bystander effect.

The following day after school, that rude boy's mate happened to be outside again, only to be greeted, so to speak, by this sixth former who was safe but hard, well known for how he handled himself and apparently was distantly related to the nose-beaten guy, and who proceeded to exact retribution. They said Rude Boy's mate took a bit of a pasting. Can't say I wasn't glad. Rude Boy, on the other hand, didn't show his face for a few days, got suspended, justice served. Just wished that it was me that was the vigilante, and not the sheep, grazing on the grass verge.

CREATINE

The air in the college canteen is thick with testosterone, like a pea soup mixed with a tub-load of creatine powder. My best mate Richard, Mo, Gareth and me are all sat around a table, on which sit seven empty Coke cans and a whole load of sweetie wrappers, the contents of which are not digesting in my stomach; they're lodged in between the train tracks and rubber-band contraptions that make my mouth look like an aerial shot of a twenty-five-car pile-up on the M1.

We're all students here, studying GNVQs, yet none of us knows what it stands for, and there's not a great deal of studying going on, 'cause there's a pool table and a *Time Crisis* arcade machine in the canteen and an alleyway round the back of the college where we smoke weed, getting hot rock burns in our hoodies, identified by the colour of the stripes on our Reebok Classics, regularly comparing notes on who got kicked in, who got fingered and who got what robbed when they were silly enough to put on a house party when their parents went away for the weekend, inviting what *were* the popular kids back in year 11 at school, until the choice between college and sixth form redefined the social hierarchies, and now here we all are, unlikely to ever pursue careers in IT or leisure and tourism, but we're all doing the course.

Wearing a grubby white Nike hat, Mo is talking about 2Pac. Now, I love music, I like hip-hop, but I don't have MTV, so I don't know that many of 2Pac's tunes, and I know for a fact that my best mate Richard knows fuck-all. And I know that he knows that I know. He has seven CDs in his collection and most of those are *Now* compilations, he buys them with the WH Smith vouchers he gets every Christmas from his nan, and the only CD in that malnourished collection of his that even comes close to 2Pac is a single of 'Boom! Shake the Room' by Will Smith. Despite that, every time Mo mentions a particular 2Pac track, Gareth, Richard and me all chime in in unison with the well-rehearsed chorus of:

'Yeah, yeah, sick, yeah.'

We don't ask questions here, we just agree. Gareth takes a last-ditch swig on his Coke and swirls it round his mouth, letting out a large burp that I can smell, and it smells of McDonald's cheeseburgers. He then reaches down into his World Dance record bag, pulling out the latest copy of *Max Power* magazine, skimming a few pages until he lands on the featured article on a souped-up maroon Vauxhall Cavalier with possibly the biggest exhaust I've ever seen.

'It's full bore,' Gareth says.

'Yeah, yeah, sick, yeah,' we all say.

And Mo does that finger snap, which I know for a fact that Richard can't do, but I know he's been practising in his bedroom and I notice his right hand twitch on the table as if he wants to, but he can't, and I wanna laugh. Gareth then goes on to tell us about his older brother's Ford Escort XR3i, which has a two-litre engine, lowered suspension and a dump valve.

'Yeah, yeah, sick, yeah,' we all say.

I don't even know what a dump valve is. Now Mo's telling us about his cousin's Clio, with a Kenwood subwoofer in the back, just like the name on the back of Gareth's black bomber jacket.

'Yeah, yeah, sick, yeah,' we all say.

Hold on, wait a minute, Richard's now talking?! He's saying he's rewired the stereo in his car?!

'Yeah, yeah, sick, yeah,' we all say.

No he hasn't! All he's done is change the default radio setting from Radio 2, 'cause it's not his car! It's his mum's Nissan Micra! And now he's saying he's playing this *sick new tape* from this sick *new Garage Nation tape pack* he bought, *EZ and MC Dapper.*

'Yeah, yeah, sick, yeah,' we all say.

It's not a tape pack! He taped it off Kiss 100, because I told him to!

'It's got bare dubplates,' he says.

Bare dubplates?! Since when did Richard talk like that?! He doesn't even know what a dubplate is!

'Yeah, yeah, sick, yeah,' we all say.

No, no, no yeah! He's not worthy of the *yeah, yeah, sick, yeah*. He's talking bollocks! But oh no, he doesn't stop, he carries on, his mouth opens and words come out.

'Oi, boys,' he says.

'Heard this sick new tune on the radio this week… it's by Travis.'

'… … … …'

'… … … …'

'… … … …'

Like a sound system limiter kicking in the conversation peaks, then with an ear-splitting frequency it suddenly cuts out! And we're left with no sound. And that silent moment quickly becomes a fast-moving dark cloud about to shroud us all in shadow and we begin to twitch, ready to whip out Nokia pay-as-you-go phones to distract ourselves (from ourselves).

'What?' says Gareth.

Travis?! I'm thinking, *Shit, Rich, what have you just gone and done?* I can't look at him, but I notice Gareth has this angry stare. My mouth is open, revealing the mangled Weapon X spectacle that is my teeth. Mo shimmies in his seat, puts his chin to his chest, then Richard speaks again.

'Yeah, you know, Travis, that tune, on the radio, it's sick, yeah? Yeah...?'

Richard pauses, then stares at the empty Coke cans. Mo pulls out his phone, but Gareth doesn't let it go.

'Travis? What, like, the indie band, with guitars and that? Don't those pussies back in sixth form listen to that?'

Now, I quite like some guitar bands, but I tend to keep that quiet unless I'm talking to my dad. Though I don't have MTV, I do know one or two of Travis's tunes, my little sister likes them, she's probably gonna go to sixth form, so I decide to throw Richard a rope. Well, more like a shoelace.

'What track is it, Rich?'

'I dunno. I think it's called, like, "Twist" or something.'

And I notice his eyes open up, a little bit, as if he's sensed a small slice of hope, but then out of nowhere Mo suddenly looks up from playing Snake on his phone and lets out an involuntary

'Turn?'

'Yeah, "Turn", that's it, that's the one!' says Richard, sitting up a little straighter now.

Surprisingly, Mo is right; there is a track called 'Turn' by Travis. I know that track, I quite like that track, it's alright.

'Yeah, I've heard that that track, Rich... quite like that track, it's alright.'

'Yeah, I've heard it too, it's alright,' says Mo.

And then all the attention turns to Gareth, who takes a brief moment before he speaks.

'Hold tight, does it go *turn turn tu-ur-ur urn-urn-ur*?'

'Yeah!' says Richard.

'Yeah, yeah... I've heard that track... it's alright... it's pretty sick actually, yeah, yeah, that track's sick.'

'Yeah, yeah, it is sick,' says Mo.

'Yeah! Really sick!' Richard replies.

'Yeah, yeah, sick, yeah,' we all say.

And for a brief and beautiful moment, all the bravado that exists between us becomes like bubbles being blown by five-year-olds at a summer garden party, and it feels like my dad's big hand rubbing my hair when I first fell off my bike and I realised everything was gonna be alright... until another dark cloud threatens to rain on the children's party in the garden, and the conversation is then very carefully manoeuvred to DJ Hype and Kenny Ken, and who our favourite jungle MCs are. And before I know it, we're back to talking about cars again, and I'm back to agreeing on things I know nothing about, and could well be complete bullshit, and probably are bullshit, and speaking of bullshit, Richard's bullshitting again! He reckons he's getting seventeen-inch alloy wheels fitted, to his mum's Nissan Micra, which, he fails to mention to the rest of the boys, has a big National Trust sticker in the back window.

'Yeah, yeah, sick, yeah,' we all say, including me.

LOST DAYS LOST

On the pavement by the car the copper boot-stamps the cherry on the cigarette flicked from the window of the Uno that we're sitting in, shitting it, scared we'll get nicked 'cause there's a big bag of weed that the copper hasn't seen

in the lights of his squad car, parked next to ours, like a product in a window illuminated by a glow. We threw it out the window when his lights were on show and now we're sitting here praying any minute that he'll go, 'cause if he sees it then he'll seize it and it cost a lot of dough; it was a quarter!

And it was worth forty squid! We're only seventeen and we're nearly always skint. We're students or we're shelf-stackers just wanting a zoot and we're too young to go in pubs and start drinking booze. And any time we do, some trouble always happens with some little goldfish who think they're North Atlantic salmon. Geezers doing pigeon chest demanding who we know, squaring up while circling are all their mates in tow.

We're only seventeen but we've been there many times, so we'd rather sit in cars, smoke some weed and have a laugh. Slagging off the music being played in the charts, playing drum and bass and garage-spitting rubbish bars. We don't mean any harm; that's why we're sitting in the dark in the PM when there's no one else around in the park.

The copper is demanding that we step out the car. He asks all of us: are we known to police? He turns to look at me and I say, 'No, sir, not me,' but in the corner of my eye I can see that bag of weed and I know my eyes are red and there's chocolate round my mouth and crisps down my jumper and my head is full of doubts. I'm afraid, and I want to run away, but I can't really run because I'm feeling pretty caned.

And now I'm actually giggling and so are my mates, when I know, on the floor, is the weed just yards away, and the copper has a torch that he's shining in my face. He's almost squaring up to me, I sense a growing rage, but instead he just says that we're free to go away and when he was our age he was 'out getting laid pulling birds every week,' and we should do the same.

We watch him get in his car, eyes half on the weed, still sitting highlighted by his headlight beams, and as he pulls away we all feel relieved! We grab the bag of weed and get back into the car. There's a moment of silence, then we all begin to laugh, and I laugh hard, but underneath the laughs my heart is beating fast like a fuel-injected car. Can't believe we got away with that. Again.

NO FRILLS

Five thousand flyers,
aliases printed on glossy A5,
names derived from comic book superheroes,
sculpted from the insecurities forming bravado,
manipulated in daydreams of suburban boredom where
bedroom
walls were adorned with posters from the big raves.

I remember we were out in the rain, me and Mick,
skipping and grinning, totally chuffed, thinking it was the
beginning of things to come.
We celebrated over a pint, we were bringing
our sound to our town, our night!
We hired the venue, put a deposit down, shook the
manager's hand, left the club and then got drenched.

Five thousand flyers
distributed to shops, colleges and takeaways,
all displaying our names.

'Who are they and who are you?' they'd say.

We grew up in a vacuum,
a bland sandwich filling between London and
Brighton where the bars and clubs regurgitated a
stream of commercial pop tracks with limited
shelf life, so we devised a scheme: to put on
our own night, bringing a slice of the
underground, that pirate radio sound, that
twist-your-aerial-round, receiving frequencies
from the big vibrant city to the small
sleepy commuter town, defying our age,
providing a platform for us and our mates.
We were DJs and MCs.
We just wanted a chance to play.
We just wanted a chance to play.

Skinny rude boys wearing crazy mosh pattern,
Nike TNs, Air Max and tight-fitting hats.

One DJ, one microphone, too many MCs, probably,
underage in a provincial wine bar half-empty, possibly
imagining they're Skibadee rapping at a One Nation rave.
We couldn't tempt many females in, apart
from girlfriends of the MCs or the DJs or
one or two rude girls, sucking up attention from the
eyeballs of the dominant males doing that funny
ritual dance, collars up and circling, shoulders hunched,
elbows out and in, jaw up and down like a pneumatic
drill in the middle of the dance floor swallowing pills.

The manager would complain about the music we'd play.
He'd say:

'I want party music, this isn't party music,
and who were those guys fighting inside and outside
and why are the police here again?'

Most months there was some sort of punch-up, petty
rivalries and rows of small towns, opportunistic MCs
wanting to grab the mic without wanting to put the
work in that went with earning a spot.

Over ten months, we learned a lot, adding our flyers with
our names to suburban bedroom walls full of the big shots.
We just wanted a chance to play
in the shadow of the city, halfway to the sea,
rubbing stones together to try and spark up a scene.
We just wanted a chance to play.
We just wanted a chance to play.

JUNGLE WARFARE

By the tender age of fourteen, I fully understood the nature of the war I was up against. I had a duty to protect the fragility of my lugholes. The gateway to my soul.

My bus journey to school was the frontline. Commercial breakfast radio was the enemy trying to infiltrate my eardrums. Even back then I used to think that all daytime radio DJs sounded exactly the same. I'd imagine they were all really just one person, broadcasting to the nation simultaneously like the voice of the Mysterons.

So I had to fight back. My chosen weapon to retaliate? A Walkman, with tape cassettes, copied from tape cassettes, copied from tape packs. One Nation, Helter Skelter, Dreamscape and Fever. Nicky Blackmarket and Stevie Hyper D at Energy '97 was the one. Me and my bus mate, one earpiece each, opposite ear covered by a hand; exterior frequencies couldn't penetrate us. Me, century position, commandeering the seat; my mate asleep. Not even a hectic Amen jungle break could keep him awake, but he was safe there nonetheless. Tuts, scowls and frowns. Occasionally, someone would turn round from the seat in front and say:

'Can you TURN that repetitive crap down?'

I'd reply as best I could:

'Sorry, but I'm fed-up with hearing Boyzone playlisted on repeat and I'm not interested in tailbacks on junction 9 of the M25, I'm fourteen years old.'

The more I listened, the deeper I delved. Lost in a world of beats, bass, MCs and DJs. Bus journey sessions expanded to include lessons whilst sitting in class. I had a mutual understanding with school: weren't really interested in school, school didn't seem interested in me. Unexpectedly, I scraped through my GCSE exams with average grades, but I had to search for knowledge and opportunities myself, carving them open with my own hands, moulding them to shape my needs, and music, music was my defence mechanism in times of need. A sonic shield. A forcefield to protect me from my enemies.

Now, I don't remember precisely when that form of defence became attack. Maybe when my brother bought a second-hand set of belt-drive turntables. To me they were like 1210s. I was on a different journey by then. College had taken over where school had left off and of course I didn't last very long, finishing before my time was due to expire.

Despite the pessimism, questions began to form in my little brain. I started to see, then believe that there could be opportunities, even for me.

I could be a DJ?
Even an MC?

I remember the day I found out Shabba D was a white guy, just like me! Except he was from London, not like me. I grew up in a small commuter town in Surrey, but excitement overruled fear and embarrassment and I belly-flopped into the deep end. The idea that I could write lyrics gave me enthusiasm that I never knew that I had! Any slice of information I could get, I grabbed. I began to write lyrics, realised I had a lot I wanted to get off my chest, realised too how hard it was. I didn't have a clue, but I persevered, trying desperately to manifest the blood, sweat and tears artists so often talk about when referring to their work. Hours spent cocooned in my bedroom. A Base shoebox quickly began to fill with backs of envelopes, card and scrap paper. It was all I wanted to do.

The generic radio DJs on the school bus were now a distant memory; Boyzone had long since split; I had a new enemy to contend with. Tacky nightclubs and pubs pumping out the same crap I'd spent years trying to shield my ears from, except this time it was harder.

There was booze.

There was girls.

Temptation almost took me off the rails. The shiny Base loafers belonging to the Base shoebox were almost permanently swapped for my trainers. Lyric writing made me prone to isolation.

Someone was testing my patience.

I decided to counteract. Fridays were dedicated to making mixtapes, one damp smoky shed cramped with me and my mates. Smoke and mix sessions in sheds and bedrooms quickly turned into house parties, then a monthly night at a local venue.

Yet still my enemies lingered. Appearing in the form of managers, supervisors and team leaders.

Stronger and harder.

Since leaving education with little but a few laughs my days were now consumed with low-paid work. Time was now more precious than ever. Gradually, I started to see friends go their separate ways; some fell by the wayside.

Man down.

Succumbing to the dull drums of uniform behaviour, commercial breakfast radio polluting the airspace of their kitchens each morning as they sipped on the bitter taste of strong coffee just to stay awake.

Me? I soldiered on. Which brings me to where I am now. The balance of power has shifted rapidly. I'm still fighting but I'm

tired from battling, hanging on to the belief that I can still win this war, struggling to keep my head above the water, swimming in the moat of the enemy's keep.

I can feel them slowly closing in around me.

Surrounded, circled, flanked at all angles, barely anywhere left to run. Daytime radio, prime-time television, glossy magazines, billboards, buses, tubes, trains and trams.

Still, I fight on.

If my earphones aren't clasped around my ears, then it's my hands, refusing to listen. If ever I'm losing the faith, I just rewind my old rave tapes, reload, and start again.

'Junglists, are you ready?'

THE IRONY OF IT ALL

Have you ever been struck by the sun?
Water absorbed into newspaper
folded and left out to dry
forms as hard as a brick, so,
when hit, a force will be
felt equivalent to a
David Haye knockout punch,
leaving one with only the irony of it all upon waking later.

I used to deliver the papers as a boy. A spectator in the rat races of neighbours. Cursing front doors with cause to order broadsheets swelling with supplements on a Sunday that would take seven days just to read. A paper chaser delivering papers in a regular routine. This monotonous cycle would see me heavily burdened on a bicycle come sun or rain for the innocent pursuit of earning petty change. The mentality of work etched into my brain from an early age.

Ever since those days, I've worked hard to stop the end from becoming the means. My capacity to daydream has allowed me to momentarily escape mundane occupations on many occasions, otherwise I'd see life as a lost cause, though I do believe in the honesty of hard work and earning a wage. My parents fed me the mantra of

'A fair day's work for a fair day's pay',

but I'd be lying if I said I hadn't ever complained, about the nature of earning a wage for companies lacking morals or simply working jobs that didn't stimulate my brain, searching for someone to blame for my predicaments until all fingers pointed towards me.

I crawled through school on my belly and upon leaving secondary learned that GCSEs were at best a test of memory, though I know I could've done better. Friends of mine that achieved and went on to study degrees, progressing to the fast lane of the career path, have earned the right to deconstruct the system they left behind along with me.

Until recently, I still felt like the kid on my burdened bike pedalling, peddling papers in the pursuit of paper by being the purveyor of news, on a conveyor belt of tail-chasing, perpetually complaining, until one day back at home my mum said to me:

'You're lucky to be living in these times.
You're the guardian of your own independence.
You've inherited everything and more from your ancestors.
Stop treading water and start swimming… and stop reading the bloody *Sun*!'

and she clipped me round the back of the head with a folded-up copy of the *Sun* I'd brought home from work. Outside it was raining. My head darted back towards the *Sun* Mum just coshed me with. *I am lucky*, I thought.

COKE CAN

They'd say that I talk too much,
they'd say that I'm falling behind,
they'd say that I drift away in class,
I'd say they were definitely right.

They'd say that I get distracted,
they'd say I'm silly but nice,
they'd say that I misbehave in class,
I'd say they were definitely right.

They'd say that I can't speak properly,
they'd say that I'm putting it on,
they'd say that I keep bad company,
I'd say they were definitely wrong .

They'd say I won't try and I'm lazy,
they say that I could do better,
they'd say I should know what I want,
I'd say they were definitely wrong.

They'd say, 'That's funny for you,'
in front of the rest of the group,
they'd say that I'm talented
in a room when it's just us two.

They'd say that I think too much,
catching flies, I don't have a clue,
they'd say that I can be so dumb
in a room when bunnin' on zoots.

They'd say I'm the butt of the jokes
in a bar when girls were around,
they'd ask me to come along with them
as a mate on a date in town.

They'd say that I won't last long
when I said that I wanna leave home,
they'd say that I'd make mistakes,
fall flat on my face in the road.

They'd say that I don't try hard enough,
they'd say at home I'm rude,
they'd say that I lack manners
at the table eating food.

They'd say that God has a plan
they'd say I should be a man
they'd say, 'What are you saying?'
when I said that I don't understand

They'd say don't answer back,
they'd say respect your elders,
they'd say your siblings did it
when talking about A-levels.

They'd say take risks,
they'd say put trust in faith,
they'd say remember your manners,
you'll find your way.

WHOEVER SAID IT WAS EASY

Getting out of bed, on time,
eating breakfast
if you're lucky,
jump in the shower,
pack your bag,
brush your teeth,

look in the mirror,
check for spots,
do your hair,

open the door,
wrap up warm,
say goodbye,
step out your house and
bop to the bus stop, all the while looking cool?
That's hard,

all of that, five
days a week
is hard.

Getting on the bus and being cussed because
your team lost the night before
or the trainers that you're wearing represent
what your mum and dad can't afford
or your jumper, shirt and trousers were what your
older brother was wearing the year before
or there's a girl sitting two seats behind you that you've
fancied for two years and you know that she has her
hair in a bun on Mondays and Thursdays, wears eye
shadow on a Friday but doesn't get the bus
home because of drama class, yet she
doesn't even know your name?
That's hard,

all of that, five

days a week
is hard.

Sitting in class, and no matter how hard you
try you just can't understand what's going on,
or you're studying so many subjects in one afternoon you get
confused,
or the pressure of hitting those high grades just to hold down
that uni place,
that's hard.

Having the answer to the one question that at
some point in your school life you will be asked:

'What do you want to be when you leave?'

To even have an inkling of an answer,
that's hard.

But what's really hard,
what is incredibly hard,
what is *University Challenge* hard
is when you know what you want,
when you know what you want to be,
whatever that may be, but
it seems everyone around
you wants to tell you
you can't,
you can't.

'You can't do that,
people like you
don't do that.
I've never done that, so
you can't do that,
you can't.'

It's as delicate as an egg, balanced on the
slight curvature of a spoon, then
placed into a race on school
sports day.

A plant trying to lay roots in shallow soil subjected to wind.

A thin plastic black and white 99p football that
makes a *ping* when kicked and goes off in the wrong
direction, floating in slow motion into a bush full of
stinging nettles, watched by a rabble of open-
mouthed young boys.

An adult robin, leaving a nest full of chicks
unattended for a split second, under the
swooping shadow of a magpie.

All because
someone says:

'White boys don't make rappers,
black boys don't make painters,
brown boys don't make footballers,
girls don't sit on boards of big business,
state school kids don't make prime ministers.'

For every one *can*, there must be about a thousand *can'ts*.
That's like a one in one thousand chance of
making a *can* an actuality.
It's like trying to hum your own tune in a packed
stadium singing a football chant.

That one *can* is still a chance and I would rather fail
knowing that I'd at least tried than give in to
the voices telling me that I can't,
and there's a lot of them,
and yes, it is hard,
but it gets
easier.

PART 2:

BELLY FLOP

LONDON CALLING

Some people see race, some people see class, some people see religion, some people see all three and make a counterfeit informed decision about your upbringing, in order to package it into a little box, gaffer-taping the flaps and placing it onto a shelf with millions of other boxes, categorised and sub-categorised with the precision of German engineering. Some boxes don't fit their space; some boxes need to find another place, whether or not it's miscellaneous; some say living is like a box, according to the box.

Outside the M25, believe it or not, life exists. Restricted to the drips from the city's residue. London's heat creates a condensation providing a smoke screen some call the suburban dream. I pricked that little bubble, because there weren't enough holes in the commuter belt to keep me from being exposed. The fire in my belly was on the verge of being extinguished, ready to relinquish any creativity and submit to a well-doctored dose of docile normality, revolving round the security of a reasonable salary, whatever's on the telly, holidays to Málaga and a small-town mentality.

I had to escape for my sanity, make a break for the city, where hostility forms the reception committee. But hostility creates, or breaks, an attitude that wants to set the pace, wants to win that race then keep on running. The fight for space keeps the fire in my belly burning; the competitive nature draws creators, innovators and paper chasers, consumers and commuters wanting a piece of the pie; opportunities arise to match the heights of living in a high-rise. In my eyes, this is where I need to be; don't know if it's where I belong but I'm here to figure that out. The heat keeps the flame from going out and when the fire's out, I'm out, ready to call it quits. Got nothing against my small-town upbringing, but for me my little box just didn't fit.

The ability to exist and not be seen, the ability to find a scene within a scene that suits your means, the ability to be seen and live some kind of dream, the ability to get on a bus and see a scene that back home you only see on a screen, the ability to witness poverty and wealth on the same street and measure the extremes, the ability to be in a city with a queen, the ability to become a fiend regardless of means, the ability in London to end every single sentence with *yeah-safe-bless-sweet-ya-get-me-still-scene*, and most people understanding what you mean, do you know what I mean? Scene.

Someone once told me that Hollywood, an apparent city of dreams, behind the scenes, can be a haven for drug addicts, prostitutes and abject poverty. For some, I understand London can be a cruel lottery; you don't know when your numbers are up. For me, whatever my luck, I know in this city I got a better chance of finding a space for my little box, whether or not it's Cardboard City or Kensington. If not, I might as well go back to my place of birth, close the flaps on my box and suffocate under the gaffer tape, consumed with bitterness about how much I don't like the place and if I was given half a chance I could've been someone. Well, enough of that. I'm up in London now; there's work to be done.

THE 21.00 TO NOWHERE

One of several large flat-screen TVs blinks silently, rotating an incessant stream of updating information from the world of football and a few other sports which fight like pigeons over the remaining crumbs of coverage, muted to a theme tune of songs played over the PA, mostly belonging to a decade before. Lip-syncing Sky Sports newsreaders with Snow Patrol or Oasis becomes a game in itself. The many pillars of unofficial knowledge that often populate pubs, normally stood like dusty ornaments at the bar, will tell you the breweries pay less to PRS for the older songs, like it's some grand racket that none of us are supposed to be in on.

This is no normal pub. Establishments like this one, with its sports screens, high bar stools and signed shirts in frames, will rarely produce such loyal patrons, due to the nature of the clientele they serve on a daily basis, for they belong in train stations. Suspending animation between places as people revolve as fast as turnstile gates on packed match days.

Located conveniently between A and B, these are the types of bars which I never remember the name of, but chances are I'll know what beers they sell, how much they charge, and I'll quietly tut when I receive my change on a shiny silver tray with a receipt including the VAT breakdown and the bartender's name, which in this case is Pascal, not that we're on a first-name basis, and it's that lack of familiarity which appeals to me.

With décor and furniture normally generic enough that even the most eccentric amongst us can blend in and become anonymous, it's in here I can quietly sip my beer and disappear. In here I don't exist, trapped between time zones for when I have no place to go. This soulless sports bar is a waiting room, where reason can consult my heart and pick apart my brain, or simply sit, sip and switch off.

I watch as commuters come and go for a post-work drink.

Some look as if they're biding their time before the big squeeze back to the provinces, towns of the type I grew up in. Tourists browse the expensive food menus in which oven-heated ready meals appear at the blink of an eye. Groups of lads and girls break journeys, downing booze at breakneck speed before they leave to presumably go on elsewhere to drink even more.

If I sit here long enough, the merry-go-round of sports updates will produce a new piece of news. I might even hear a song I once liked. The few pound coins in the tray, the residue of a £10 note used to pay for a pint, may not even see the dark cotton cushion of my pocket, and may just be popped into the slot of a fruit machine, depending on how low I sink.

Today I'm sat, about three feet off the ground, on this high stool, nursing an expensive pint poured by Pascal, and I will take my time. This bar is my camo-pattern jacket hidden amongst the leaves and, when I'm ready, I'll slowly slip off my stool and go locate my train.

MONTAGE

You wake up,
you walk into the bathroom,
you're wondering what's happened to your mate,
your best mate.
What's changed?
You ain't seen him in days.
You look in the mirror and wonder what's happened to your face.
What's changed?
You ain't shaved in days.
Another line in your forehead appears,
the gears in your imagination begin to grind,
the light in your mind flickers and the film reels begin to rotate.

Cue montage.
Coldplay plays,
your mate and his girl,
arm-in-arm walks in the park kicking up leaves,
feeding ducks in the pond,
trips to the sea,
trips to art galleries,
joint shopping trips to Gap and H&M,
his and hers, hers and his,
sharing friends over drinks,
mates are now friends, friends are now
ours, ours ain't his, ours ain't you,
dinner parties, dinner parties using
recipes taken from celebrity chefs, expensive
A4 hardback conveniently rests on the clinically clean
kitchen surface, strategically placed to make it look like it wasn't placed to imply taste,
Sunday afternoons in gastropubs or in Starbucks, drinking from huge coffee mugs held with two hands, then taking selfies,
cheesy trinkets and cutlery,
amalgamating diaries,

middle-ground CDs,
middle-ground DVDs,
middle-ground being,
feeling like carpet under your feet, hiding the
cold hard damp scarred floorboards underneath where
skeletons of single ex-friends lie recluse
for choosing to refuse to wear shoes in place of trainers
in order to gain entry into cheesy nightclub venues,
continuing to smoke weed, consume lager, watch
football and smash kebabs,
still listening to hip-hop and underground dance music,
still rebelling against chart music,
still laughing when farting,
still openly honest about porn use,
still treading water in an ocean of self-loathing where the
only humane feeling that remains is the pain from
getting salt in the wounds,
still complaining about the day-to-day pursuit of pay and
feeling unfulfilled, that grates like an itch you can never
quite reach between the shoulder blades,
lacking the kind of companion that will scratch it and
relieve it, then embrace you for all your insecurities,
idiosyncrasies and imperfections and tell you that it will all be
OK,
chuckling in your ear, stroking your hair, kissing you
on the cheek, then walking away, leaving her sweet
perfume in the airspace as you look in the mirror, see
your face, think of her and think, *Shit,*
life's alright.

Instead you see your face,
your muggy unshaven face,
and you think of your mate
and you hope the prick is happy.

MARIA

Maria worked on the checkouts, she served me the day I had my interview. Her natural blonde hair highlighted by a coat of peroxide, like a picture within a painting. Her brown eyes and round suntanned face were scarred with a plaster just above the top left of her lip, covering a piercing deemed unacceptable by the management. She used to wear this perfume which made my nostrils anxious any time she wasn't there.

We got talking one evening, when she was relieved from her till during a quiet hour and sent to assist me stacking the shelves. I knew I liked her as soon as we started talking, because my lips went from a state of being unable to form sentences to suddenly pebble-dashing words in desperate attempts to hold her attention and make me sound interesting. I just came across as a gibbering wreck, barely able to stand due to my knees wanting to give way, as my stomach was simulating the kind of sensations I'd only ever had riding the Vampire ride at Chessington. She told me she liked drum and bass, and hip-hop, and she wrote poetry! I told her I was an MC and I was trying to convey to her my frustrations about other MCs, who didn't know when to stop rapping and let the music breathe, and that I wasn't one of them, I knew when to stop, I weren't no motormouth and I rapped at half the speed like hip-hop, but I lacked that confidence those rude boys had, that arrogant swagger, the type which attracted girls.

As an MC, every time I went to perform, or any time I tried to talk to a girl that I liked, it was like a pack of pit bulls were circling the perimeters of my fears whilst I sat on a carousel, repeatedly riding it round and round, wishing I could just jump off and make a break for it in some recurring fairground nightmare. I couldn't concentrate on anything I was doing, my nerves were corrupting all reason, I placed a baked bean tin on a shelf full of shampoo and didn't even notice until she corrected me, laughing.

These conversations continued over a period of weeks. I'd begin every shift with a wish that she was working too, savouring every second of speech, begging for minutes more. She was interesting. She read books, painted and wrote poems, and she was gorgeous. I didn't know girls like this existed. She worked in the evenings and was the only part-timer who didn't work Saturdays; she said she needed her Friday nights for raving.

Though we talked a lot, I wasn't really getting the impression that she was into me and I was hopelessly floating into friendship, a fate that I'd suffered before, made even worse by the news she broke to me one evening that she was leaving to go to art college.

That night back at the bedsit, I was drinking a cup of tea, listening to music, thinking about points in the past where I thought I'd let myself down, and there were quite a few. I decided I weren't gonna let this one slip away like all the others, I had to say something, I had to tell Maria I liked her, and ask her out. I could hear those pit bulls barking but I was prepared to risk getting bitten.

Something must have been right, because the next day I found out from my friend Anthony, who also worked on the checkouts, that her final shift coincided with the one day of the week I was working a late. On the final day, she wasn't due in till four and would finish at seven; I was starting at twelve and working till eight. I knew my window of opportunity would be small, so I had to be ruthless. I worked out what I was gonna say the night before in the bedsit and this looped round my head all day long, disturbing the delicate network of needle-threads that was my nervous system, but I remained determined. I was gonna kick those pit bulls right in the balls and if they bit, then so be it. At least I would have tried.

I didn't get to see Maria arrive that day. An unusual influx of customers kept both me and her busy for what would normally be a quiet evening, once the post-work rush was over. Any spare moment I got was spent hoping she'd come off her checkout and come and work with me filling up the freezers. Any quiet moment, though, was brief and was soon disturbed by queues of flippin' customers.

When I checked the clock for the first time, it was already gone six. I knew time was running out and I was beginning to lose the plot when I likened myself to Keanu Reeves in *Speed*, on speed, as my behaviour started to become more frantic. At quarter to seven, fifteen minutes left, hauling a cage full of booze too fast around a corner I tipped it over and smashed a whole crate of beer on the shop floor! By the time I'd run upstairs to the warehouse to get a bucket, mop and dustpan, then dealt with a complaint from a customer and proceeded to unload the cage that I should have already dealt with, it was ten past seven! I went straight to the checkouts, then ran upstairs to the warehouse, the canteen and the office, but I just could not find her. An announcement then went up for her to return to the checkouts, but she never appeared; she was gone.

I went back to the aisle where the booze was and began filling the shelves like I was supposed to. I was never really one to skive off or break rules, and of course by now the shop had pretty much emptied and I was on my own. I'd missed my chance. Twenty-one and I'd still hadn't cracked the code. I'd let a few go before without saying a thing and regretted it, but this one was gonna hurt. Maria was something else. I'd not met a girl like her before. She wore white and red Air Force 1s and liked hip-hop and drum and bass! I thought that I was probably punching above my weight anyway; most of the other guys who worked there fancied her. What was I thinking? Failure had become an all-too-reoccurring theme, as if it was prewritten in my DNA.

For no particular reason, probably just looking for some *Dawson's Creek* moment of enlightenment, I stood looking at the expensive whiskeys in the glass cabinet, until I caught my own reflection. I saw that blue Sainsbury's shirt with my orange name tag, a shaved head with a high-fade, complete with the eight-carat trimmings of a chain, earrings and a bracelet, all the exterior hallmarks of a small-town wide boy applied to an all-too-familiar face, and I quickly looked away.

I stayed standing, staring at the rest of the booze on the shelves, then turned round to the front of the store, where I could see past the checkouts, through the big glass windows, to the street drinkers outside, sat in the bus shelters and on the pavement, swigging on them big bottles of cheap cider and Tudor Rose, and I decided that I'd be better off if I just concentrated on getting the simple things right, like getting all the labels on the whiskey bottles aligned and facing front. I had to take this one on the chin. I was pretty sure it's what my dad would have said.

The bottles on the top shelf took a bit of reaching to rearrange, so I had to get up on my tiptoes. After bringing my arms back down from a stretch, out of nowhere, my peripheral vision suddenly picked up movement to my left and my heart pitch shifted up a couple of beats. As I turned round to face the cage at the end of the aisle, it was like that very moment when the Vampire ride reaches the pinnacle of the incline and then drops! There she was! Standing next to the cage that only minutes ago I'd tipped over, wearing her own clothes, she'd changed out of the shapeless Sainsbury's uniform and into a denim combo that kissed her curves. She'd let her blonde hair down, which was now brushing against her shoulders. She walked towards me and I could not move, stunned into silence. I remember noticing my mouth was wide open but there was nothing I could do. Before I could even contemplate producing a sound, she took the lead. She said she hadn't seen me, and wanted to say goodbye and give me this, placing a piece of paper into my hand. Written on it was her name, her mobile number, and a kiss. She then backed away with a smile and said:

'Ring me.'

The only words I managed were:

'Er, alright.'

I stood there for God knows how long until I finished my shift. My friend Anthony came up to me just as I was leaving and asked me if Maria had spoken to me. I said:

'Yeah! ...Hold on, wait a minute, what, you knew?'

And he said to me:

'Mate, everyone did.'

I walked back down London Road that night like there were fuel injections in my feet, a subwoofer in my stomach and a massive spoiler attached to the back of my shoulder blades. I bowled past the street drinkers and students, through the viaduct and back up to the bedsit. I felt fully in the moment. It might not have been me that did it, but those pit bulls were put to sleep.

A PALE SHADE OF WHITE

This one time I sold out.

Imagine a drawstring bag being pulled tight.
That's what my skin felt like, bathed in waves of ultraviolet light.
The extreme temperature was, like, twice the intensity of any pressure
inflicted on me by sections of society obsessed with image, or any
mates teasing me with well-worn-out white jokes, or people
who I barely know having the bollocks to tell me I
shouldn't wear shorts.

My mate from the office used to go, so I thought I'd give it a go too.
Me and him weren't the same, though; in a
lucky dip from the gene pool I came out
Celtic, and he came out Latino.

The lady at the desk told me the minimum
amount of time was six minutes. She
looked at me and set the machine for two.

A healthy, plump piece of bacon, placed
under the naked flame of a grill, shrinks,
crackles and spits, taking on a form that
I'm quite sure nature didn't intend.

I walked out of there, almost as white as I went in, feeling
like I'd sacrificed my soul to a skint demigod
offering a pyramid scheme to bronze skin.

When my mates found out, I breathed in and
crossed my fingers for an early winter.

SMALL TALK

The geezer on my right is wearing a scarf; it's the height of the summer. The girl on my left is a PR exec, for some... PR company. My attention span diminished as soon as the first two syllables were delivered from her lips. We're all at a house party, we've just met.

PR Girl holds a bottle of rosé. My bum-cheeks are slowly slipping into the sink, perched on the edge of the kitchen surface. Scarf Boy has one of those big bottles of upmarket cider. A minute ago he was opening cupboards looking for a glass to pour it into. I would love it if the scarf dipped into the glass without him noticing.

PR Girl and Scarf Boy seem to be hitting it off. Scarf Boy has already told us he runs four times a week, 10K at a time. PR Girl has apparently started running; she's gone as far as purchasing some 'proper trainers'. Any money that, despite proclaiming she's bought all this expensive gear, she's too lazy to get off her arse and actually do it, yet she will still insist on wearing the trainers to work, with her office attire, creating the illusion of a fitness fanatic at the expense of looking ridiculous, in one of western society's most horrendous mismatches.

Scarf Boy is of an athletic build, about six foot two, his hair colour a light brown, immaculately waxed with not a strand out of place, even though everything looks out of place. His hair matches the generic colour of these instant IKEA kitchen units. Underneath his woolly purple scarf is a tight-fitting pink T-shirt; emblazoned on the front is some made-to-look-faded emblem of an American high school sports team.

PR Girl has on a dress resembling a sari and Scarf Boy has tribal tattoos, clawing out from underneath the sleeves of his tight-fitting pink T-shirt. Look past the fake tan and bronzer, clothing and tattoos from far-flung places and they both seem about as cultured as a blank piece of paper. And they're probably looking down at me! I might not pronounce all my t's, haven't been to uni and still wear Air Max, but I'm quite sure I could point out Fiji on a map and I ain't even been there! I bet they have, on a gap year.

'You alright there? You look troubled.'

Shit. PR Girl is talking to me. I think quick.

'Who, me? Yeah, I'm alright. I think I'm slipping into this sink.'

PR Girl looks about thirty. Probably twenty-five. Long straightened hair, blonde highlights. Naturally chubby but quite pretty, though her personality suggests she's as frustratingly boring and bland as a party political broadcast delaying the start of *Football Focus*.

'We wouldn't want to come in and rescue you, now.'

What's PR Girl trying to do?! Rescue me?! From the sink?! Any money she's got a membership to some swanky gym with a massive swimming pool, owns a whole load of expensive gear yet—

'Don't worry, fella, I'm trained as a lifeguard.'

Scarf Boy?! Is Scarf Boy trying to mug me off in front of PR Girl?! Lifeguard! Who's this prick think he is? Look at the state of him, straight out the Next catalogue. Scarf Boy is as boring and as bland as PR Girl. They should do PR for bland brands of scarves sold in airport departure lounges. They were made for each other.

'Nah, you're a'right, bruv, I got my swimming badge in the Cub Scouts.'

PR Girl laughs. 'Ave that, Scarf Boy, one-one, the quick equaliser. Weren't expecting that, now, were ya?

Scarf Boy tees himself up again, looking as if he's going straight back on the counter-attack:

'Yeah? I was in Cub Scouts too. You know what, I was that sad I actually went on to join Marine Cadets.'

Marine Cadets, Scarf Boy, you should have said. I was in Marine Cadets. I reply:

'Yeah… ditto, mate. I trod the same path. Cub Scouts through to Marine Cadets. It was progress. I liked it… it was a… laugh.'

Damn. Scarf Boy caught me off guard. PR Girl don't know where to look now.

'I was in Brownies, hee hee.'

Shut up, PR Girl, you're out your depth. Keep talking, Scarf Boy, I'm interested. He speaks again:

'Yeah, I loved it. Well, I liked all the running round in bushes and getting camouflaged. I weren't too fussed about all the discipline, though: marching, keeping your uniform clean. There was quite a lot of bullying, looking back.'

Wow. Scarf Boy has made me forget my sink-sore arse; I'm now trawling through memories I've not visited since the middle of my teens. I speak:

'Yeah, it was the same for me, mate. I left because I couldn't stand the demands anymore. I was fourteen or fifteen, being shouted at like I was actually in the Royal Marines. I think they forgot that it was supposed to be fun.'

Do you know what? Maybe Scarf Boy wasn't mugging me off. He seems a'right… and it can get a bit cold outside in the summer; it is England, after all. Maybe he wears the scarf to keep himself warm? He looks at both PR Girl and me when he speaks again:

'I totally agree, fella. I think with me, in the end I realised it just wasn't for me, you know? I wanted to go on lads' holidays full of British people, no culture, chips with all my meals. Look at my tattoos; I got these done when I was eighteen in Ibiza! To be honest with you, though, I'm just a big girl's blouse, really. I mean, look at me; I'm wearing a scarf indoors, for Christ's sake. Anyway, it was lovely to meet you both. Good luck with the running, Claire. My girlfriend is in this house somewhere. I'd best go find her.'

It's just me and PR Girl now. Maybe I was being a bit harsh with her. Oi, she's actually quite fit.

'So, Claire. You went to Brownies, I went to Cubs, we should, like, get together for a drink sometime and talk about it. It could be a laugh!'

PR Girl twiddles her bottle of rosé, then returns a wave to some unknown face out in the hallway, and without even looking at me she says:

'I don't think so.'

THE 12

'Shut ya mout', rude boy,'
said the man on the 12 bus,
talking to himself.

SHE SAYS

Sat on a cold, hard, shapeless plastic
chair in a sterile hotel corridor which
smells of damp towels disinfected of life.
Sipping on tasteless tea, brought from an
overpriced machine, whilst the love of your
life is in the wedding suite, sipping on champagne,
making love to a man with bigger muscles but
not much else to say.

You tell yourself he's alright and you're happy for
her whilst pretending you can't hear the high-
pitched moans which fracture the fine wine-
glass rim of your feelings and the low-
frequency mumbles like earthquake
tremors to the very structure of
your manhood, because when
she's done, you're giving her a
lift home like you always
do, because you're friends,
she told you so and
you agreed.

GIFTWRAPPED

There's some things I've never done, like watching a blood-red sunset whilst keeping her warm, or walking across a beach arm in arm, picture perfect. I might not be much of a romantic, but that time we had a cup of tea in Clapham Junction was nice, and I don't like drinking tea in those sterile coffee chains, it never tastes right, but that day it was alright.

She drank this coffee, with a beehive of cream on the top, which she somehow managed to avoid getting on her chin, with all the elegance of Audrey Hepburn, yet still remaining so down to earth. It was one of those rare occasions when she dropped her guard. We just talked, relaxed and laughed in the eye of an early-evening commuter storm, equalising all negative forces surrounding us.

There's a past between us which almost saw us together, but it never happened. And now there's a present, where we occasionally discuss what could have been. If only I'd said something before, instead of choosing to keep my mouth closed for fear of losing a friend. She says she felt the same, but those moments of honesty are like a species of butterfly rarely seen, because she conceals her feelings in shiny paper, giftwrapped with precision. I'm convinced that hidden underneath the glossy exterior lies a gift that when opened will need handling with care. It may well not be me who gets to peel off the many paper layers, but whoever it is will need patience, because she doesn't open easily.

These days I tiptoe blindfolded around her, not knowing where I stand, nor wanting to make a mistake. It was too late when I eventually tried the direct approach and I walked away, accepting my rejection like a World Cup runner-up medal, knowing I'd got so close. It wasn't what I'd wanted, but I felt I could finally begin the long walk down the road of moving on. Until whispers started tickling my ears of anger when I started seeing someone else. Things were said to others that were never said to me. It was frustrating and soon enough I was back scratching at the present under the tree, wondering if Christmas will ever come. I just don't get an answer.

When we meet, for the most part it's fun, I enjoy her company, though she nearly always exits first, as if she's stage managing her own anxieties, whilst mine take on the role of a theatre critic, harshly analysing every word of my own performance.

I would walk away and draw a line under it all if I knew one hundred percent where I stood, so I could see how hard I'd fall if it all went wrong, but I just can't let go.

Sometimes when we speak, I feel this spark if I say something to make her laugh and she flushes a little red in the cheeks. Her head moves to the left in embarrassment, then on cue her eyes open up, lighting a promenade across her face. The white cliff smile completing the perfect portrait which hangs in the gallery inside of my head. I lie awake at night visualising these pictures, a Sistine Chapel inside the roof of my skull.

I've never considered myself much of a romantic, but unless she opens up I can't unravel anything, and right now all I want, more than ever, is to have my mind at peace. I need the sleep.

EMBANKMENT

'I was, like, so drunk?'
said the well-dressed young lady
stood on the platform.

PLASTICS

In the cinders of burnt bridges I'm scared to grow anything.
The unconscious pyromaniac strikes another match,
intends to light a candle, burns down the flat,
face to flames, hands up,
ties hands, turns around,
retreats to shadows, back to flames,
looks over shoulders, *not again*.

ONFETTI

mperature of her
bottom of the station
y hands on the tops of her
f perfection that would have
on any degree of London's volatile
thermometer, red-carpeting the path towards that first kiss.
That moment was a ship worthy of splitting Tower Bridge.
My rationality stepped down and bowed to an ancient
force a thousand times the power. All unnecessary
thought slipped away, like a spacecraft discarding its
redundant superstructure, a separation I'd rarely
experienced. I spent the rest of the evening
wishing it could have lasted and worrying
about what I might've ruined, trying to
catch every shred of confetti that
was the memory.

PRIORITIES

I sit drinking my tea trying not to think; it's futile. Mechanically spun, I'm dizzy. She leads, I follow. Reading and rereading every text and email I've ever received, regarding her and me.

Sat on my black leather chair by my bed, laptop on my legs, leaning forward so my back bends and eventually hurts, phone in my left hand, tea in my right. The only thing missing is a desk and a bedroom that looks and feels like a bedroom, rather than a storage space for cardboard boxes and crates, stacked in corners, and letters from the bank, strewn across the floor with yesterday's clothes. Still, my trainers look nice, though: box-fresh Nikes, parked by my bed like a Porsche in the drive at a dive of a home. Priorities.

Back living with my parents, again. I feel sorry for them. Sleeping in the room on the other side of the wall. Twenty-seven and I can't see the feet I'm supposed to stand on. I'm sure my dad is proud. My mum worries, I worry, I'm worried now, though not for the fact that I lack employment, prospects and a pension; it's because I'm stressing about her. Priorities.

I look at my mug and just about make out my face's reflection, wondering which face is staring at a mug. Bring up an email. Take a gulp of my tea. Her few words on the screen ask more questions of me.

Busy right now, talk next week.

Not even a question, a statement. I'm worried I've stepped in the ring with someone twice my weight and punching range. Paranoia breeds every time she speaks, spreading like the mould on the bedroom walls. I'm trying to second-guess her tactics; she's like José Mourinho and route one is all I know. She's capable of switching the way she plays at any given moment, raising and lowering my hopes, like an erratic day on the stock exchange, with the tone of her voice, or the lack of syntax in an email or a text message.

It's as if she mechanically controls the mental mechanisms responsible for manufacturing paranoia, as chemicals lose their balance inside my brain, as I drunkenly walk, slip, run, then riot naked (apart from my trainers) down the neural pathways screaming out her name until my lungs hurt and I'm sprawled out on the kerb, with dirt on my brand new Nikes.

Mum is calling me from downstairs.

'It's dinner time,' she shouts.

I'm not done rereading my emails and texts! Analysing them to death.

'Ah! For God's sake, give me five minutes, Mum!'

Priorities.

NORTHERN LINE

'Bruv, Northern line, yeah?'
asked the drunk man on the tube,
District to Richmond.

YOUR NAILS

There's no way
in for now.

It's cold.

Until I see a
lightbulb colour the
air from the other side of
the door, I'll sit, wait and
measure success by the length
of your arm.

At least I know your nails look nice.

TURBO BREEZE

The pub garden is busy.
Bobble-jumpered young twenties types are
smiling, laughing and speaking loudly,
defying the cold November air, gripping
pints and glasses of wine like it's a Friday.

'Do these people actually have jobs or what?' I say.

She doesn't reply.
I've not been in this pub with her before,
yet it feels like an annual trip to an arrogant
relative who's that bit more successful.

We're sat on the wrong side of the bench,
she's staring at the fence at the back of the garden.
I'm looking at her.
Left leg crossed over right in light blue denim, handbag
still hooked over left shoulder, sitting
on the waist-length well-fitted black leather jacket,
she looks good.
She always does.

Her glass of red wine is half-full and
has been for the last twenty minutes.
I finish my drink, put the glass down on the bench and
wipe my mouth.
That was my fourth pint of premium Dutch lager.
I drank my four pints at premium speed
on an empty tummy and
I'm starting to speak double Dutch.
What feels like a million bubbles of gas has
now expanded my belly, all
that sugar has sent a power surge to my
head and I'm now overloading with words like
Ceefax gone wrong on screen.
It's a mistake I've made what seems like a
thousand times and more.

In the stick-slim gaps between sentences I
cover my mouth to burp.

I'm seasick,
drinking too quick.
My reasoning is
if there's beer between my lips
it keeps my mouth from making amateur rescue attempts in
the choppy waters of uncomfortable silences.

My body leans in towards her,
my hands are frantic as I speak.
I tell her how much I like her,
how much she means to me and
that I know this speech has been on repeat and I repeat it
every time she sees me but I mean it, I really mean it.

'I know,' she says.

Sat upright, her body is positioned away from me,
she doesn't look at me,
she barely moves.
I'm trying to make sense of this, by
drastically paddle-splashing makeshift sentences,
but her ears are waterproof.
My mouth moves like a seal pup pursued by a shark.

'Fuck's sake,' I say

under my breath, as I finish speaking and
just look at the fence.

The bell for last orders rings and she makes her excuse to leave.
We've maintained our roles,
normal service resumed.
I speak too much,
she doesn't say enough and I'm
left with a frustration so familiar I've given it a name,
guaranteed the foreseeable future will be
spent bar-brawling with the idea
that it's the same for her.

I wait five minutes till she's gone,
cover my mouth, lean forward and
let out another gassy burp.
I pick myself up and walk out the
pub, wobbling from the waves a distant
cruise ship made, bailing the
water out the lifeboat, then
heading home.

INFANT

We were sat in his living room when my mate said that she said I need to man up. I leaned forward like my torso fainted. A familiar feeling slowly stirred in my gut, like the biscuit sludge in the bottom of the mug I was holding. I looked at my mate; he shrugged his shoulders, looking like behind his dignified gaze was a smile, armed with a feather, trying to tickle the empathy currently shaping his facial structure. I wondered why she was even talking to him in the first place. I then looked away, and took my gaze back towards the mug, which had the number *25* and some badly fading balloons surrounding it, like a fancy-dress shop long since gone out of business.

I gripped the mug and bit my bottom lip. I wanted the right of reply, right there, with her in the room, with a vice-like grip on her attention and the tall concrete borders of her mind open to my side of the accusation.

Staring at my mate's carpet, whilst he played on the Xbox, I thought about what I'd talk about: the birds, the bees and the man-to-man chats they seem to have on American TV programmes that I never had; the constant doubt stood on permanent parade inside of my head, like the ticket inspector at the station who was there any time I tried to bunk the train; the feelings I felt at school any time I liked a girl my own age, the guilt and the shame, the fear of hell's flames; the names I was called before an NHS orthodontist was able to make my teeth look straight, after enduring a four-year wait in which the girls that I fancied either got pregnant or went on to study A-levels, flying rapidly out of my league.

'She just wants you to take a little more control, bruv,' my mate said, showing me a bit more of his teeth.

'Mate,' I said. 'I'd need to swing a wrecking ball through that barrier she puts up, and no one I know has got a licence. Any time I approach she goes as cold as an ATM rejecting my debit card, when I know there's money on it.'

He shrugged his shoulders again. I continued.

'Is this playing hard to get? If it is, I don't get it! I don't understand the rules; it's too complicated! I displayed my cards and I chased; ain't that what I'm supposed to do? How many glass doors do I need to keep running into before I really do get brain damage?'

I took the last gulp of my tea, and the soggy residue from a stewed teabag and what was once a proud chocolate digestive, which had disintegrated in the heat of the liquid, entered my mouth like dog shit slotted through the letter box. I continued.

'All this broken heart talk is bollocks, it's my brain that's breaking! I get brain ache any time I think about her, and I think a lot! *Man up*? I don't even know what the fuck that means anymore!'

'Women, bruv,' my mate said.

'Yeah, very insightful,' I replied. 'By the way, did she say anything else?'

Suddenly looking back at my mate again, who pressed pause on the Xbox controller, put it down on the carpet, then took a quick dunk of his biscuit into his tea, had a sip, and said:

'Yeah, yeah, she did, bruv. She wants you to stop writing those poems about her. She fucking hates it!'

ALL THIS ABOUT BROKEN HEARTS

It's like not making the school football team after putting in the performance of a lifetime in the trials and having the manager drop hints via little compliments that you'd maybe just make it.

It's like being the mate of the mate who always had the girlfriend at the cinema or in the shopping centre, sitting on the bench, realising you've run out of pick 'n' mix to distract yourself with while they kiss.

It's like waiting for a passport with only days left before you're due out on the holiday that you've been saving for, only to find out a postal strike has been called.

It's like indiscriminately offering someone out, in front of your mates, and getting dropped down in one punch, the pain of your brain shaking inside the skull upon meeting the cleanest connection of fist to face that you never saw coming.

It's like repeatedly being sick, several times in one night, and on the seventh retch, when there's nothing left but bile burning your throat, with barely enough energy for the stomach muscles to convulse, it's the knowledge that it will happen again, in a matter of minutes.

I don't get all this about broken hearts; the heart is just a muscle. All I know is that this, whatever it is, it's painful.

THE 159

'It's real out 'ere, fam,'
said the boy into his phone,
back seat of the bus.

CEMENT LEGS

It's cold outside, it's Sunday night, *Songs of Praise* time. It's dark too, skint-pocket dark. I've spent a fair few Sunday evenings of my adult life feeling pretty wretched. Hungover from the night before and the night before that. Sleep-deprived and wriggling from a rash of paranoia calling me all sorts of nasty names. Moping about, self-loathing on a sofa with about as much vitality as a squashed Ginsters pasty hanging out the back pocket of some jeans strewn carelessly across a bedroom floor.

Right now, I'm hot. Sweating, actually. I'm feeling pretty good. I just ran a few miles. I like running. Sometimes when I'm running, I just seem to stop thinking; my head goes quiet, like the M23 on Christmas Day. I enjoy the feeling of my legs carrying my body and my cold breath breathing air into my lungs. The consistency calms me, because I tend to think a lot.

You know I think a lot, and just now I was thinking about us. How those few moments I had with you was like one of them dreams, where I'm being chased. There's a mad man, wielding something sharp, or there's mad men, wielding something sharp, or that reoccurring Alsatian from down the street, charging up the pavement, rapidly making up the ground. I can feel the fuel-injected adrenaline bobsleighing round my veins, it's one of them life-or-death situations, I know what I need to do, but my legs won't move! I know what I want to do, I know what I'm supposed to do, but my legs – won't – move! I don't care what *Hollyoaks* says, or what the lads' mag says, or what the kid with the latest trainers and the football manager dad said; my legs – won't – move.

And I don't know why. It's partly why I like to write. It's only now that I realise that you didn't have the time to help me answer that question, and why should you?

You used to roll your eyes every time I used one of my football metaphors. Maybe I should look to some other sports, maybe even read more, but those moments with you were like my left foot. I can work on it, I can improve it, but it's never gonna kick like my right. It's never gonna hit that sweet curler into the top corner of the net. The best I can do is play it safe and not put myself into situations where I'm just not equipped to deal with it. Not anymore.

I don't think you're looking to pour water for a Claude Makélélé to carry; you want that tall centre-back, captain's armband, leading the line, winning every header, strong in every challenge. I'm not him, I get that. I can laugh with the boys, I can make the boys laugh, but I'm not him. I know that. I know that you know that, more than I ever knew that.

The kid with the latest trainers, football manager dad and holidays to Florida probably figured it out in the corridors between the floors of one of them cheesy nightclubs you only get in provincial towns, or in the student union, in between dancing to the *Baywatch* theme tune. That's probably how he was supposed to do it, and if he did it, fair play to him. I didn't. I tried, but my legs wouldn't move. And I don't know why; it's partly why I like to write.

You didn't have the time, but I understand that now. It's alright. I'm alright. I just ran, and I'm feeling pretty good.

PART 3:

WHEN IT ALL STOPPED MAKING SENSE

MORDEN SUNRISE

Coming down the hill it rises from behind the many-storeyed concrete curves of Merton's Civic Centre, like a massive satsuma slowly slipping into the morning pool and painting the ripples yellow, orange and red. To the immediate left, the Mostyn park sparkles, London's towers in the distance like candles on a cake; take a breath and blow.

CROWS

The internet said *en masse* they're called a murder.
I'm murdering time, on the bench on the
common, sat clocking the crows
bossing the green, on the
grass and in the trees,
keeping the parakeets
in check.

They move like a squadron, pepper-
potting across the common,
communicating in crow
speak, speaking about
me perhaps.

The internet said they recognise faces. I
wonder if they notice I've been
reading this book for the
last six weeks.

Yesterday I experimented, got in amongst them on the grass
with a bag of BBQ Hula Hoops. Within a few carefully
executed movements, they surrounded me. I got
scared and did that half-fast-walk, half-
run like I'm trying to clench my bum
cheeks under pressure whilst
rushing to catch a bus.

This morning I heard them in the tree outside my house, going
mental like pillheads in them nineties warehouse raves,
blowing on them plastic horns.
On the internet I'd read about these so-called crow courts and
I wondered if that's what all the noise was,
when the noise just
stopped.

It suddenly occurred to me that the murder might have
murdered and what had that poor crow

done to deserve it?

Sat on the bench again and I'm watching them watching
me. I think they know that I've been reading about
them on the internet, though maybe they
don't know that I'm no
threat, I'm just curious,
unemployed and
bored of
humans.

RHYTHM

It's in the teacher
side-stepping out of time at the school disco.

It's in the readership of the
Daily Mail, the *Guardian* and *Nuts* magazine.

It's in the neighbours
complaining about the noise.

It's in the belly of the binge drinkers,

the senior citizens on Saga holidays in Bognor Regis.

It's in the airwaves of a Radio 4 discussion.

It gets played daytime on Heart FM.

It's in the rails of an M&S end-of-a-season sale.

It's in the petrol of a people carrier sat in a
half-term traffic jam somewhere on the M1.

It's in the privileges of politicians,

the halls of Eton,

the tax return of a corporation
show-jumping through loopholes.

It's in the church, the Bible and it reverberates around
Canterbury cathedral.

It's in the GCSE syllabus for English literature.

It's in the cogs of industry,

the skyscrapers of financial districts,

the digits on spreadsheets typed by apathetic data entry clerk temps hungover from the night before.

It's in company client databases,

bland food, cups of tea and any exotic meal ordered with chips.

It's in the sick of a drunk teen on holiday with his mates in Málaga.

It's poured into pints in undersubscribed working men's clubs up north.

It's in the shattered fragments of a pint glass lobbed at a pub jumbo screen upon England being made to look like an amateur team and getting knocked out of another international football tournament, round two penalties.

It's in the knitting needles of the Women's Institute, the badges of a Cub and the sash of a Brownie.

It's in the tones of those who wish to tut at what they don't understand or have never had the bollocks to try,
just an arse to sit on and a mouth to criticise.

It's in the pain of those who've never had a chance,
just an ill-fitting collar that grips tight around the neck.

It's in my bones, any time I think about that second Amen break on that 'Acid Trak' by Dillinja and I screw up my face,

and it's in the prisoner, banging repetitions of unheard dissent.

STATIONS OF THE CROSS

South London's in a rush, but this double-decker bus ain't heading anywhere fast, navigating the streets with the speed of a dial-up connection trying to download every episode of *The Sopranos*. It's around nine o'clock on a winter's evening, it's raining, it's packed, it's noisy and I'm hot.

The windows are all steamed up. Reminds me of the school bus. It brings a little smile to my face when I think about me and my mate using the condensation as our paint, fingertips for brushes and each other's smirks for inspiration, drawing a big dick and balls into the window while we laughed, every time we did it, and the girls in front, of which one was the one that I'd fancied for what seemed like a lifetime of about two terms, drew hearts marked with their initials next to the initials of boys two years above.

But back to this bus. The geezer sat next to me is a big dude, not allowing me enough room to remove my jacket but just enough to slip my hand in the pocket of my wet jeans sticking to my legs and pull out my phone. Nope. She's not replied. I sigh. She's certainly not the first of any first dates that haven't made it past the pilot.

For once in my life, I decide that there is no point thinking about the why; I just close my eyes and slide into my seat. I've been on this journey before, many times; I know where it goes,

but I can feel it slowly coming on, like watching a big merchant ship from the cliffs coming in to dock. I greet the feeling like a familiar face that I don't particularly like, yet I've learned to live with. Slowly infusing in my stomach is a teabag filled with melancholy, turning my water a murky shade of inertia.

I slouch a little further into my seat and open my eyes. I can't see out the window anymore; it's too steamed up. I think we're in Brixton. I can hear raised voices in the street below and cars are beeping. The big geezer next to me is now sleeping; I can hear him breathing heavily.

The relentless conversations around me have all merged into one incoherent noise, with several tones. I imagine all the words are like heavy raindrops, spattering the glass of my very own pope-mobile, in which I'm curled up in the foetal position, trying to hide from view, drawing a dick and balls in the window using my breath, hoping everyone is too busy cheering to notice.

I pull out my phone again. Still no reply. I close back my eyes and try and think about what I'm gonna eat when I get home,

but it's no use, I'm thinking about the why, and every other why that ever was a why, and still is a why. Thinking back to last night, it was a classic case of me talking too much, again. I overdid it with the questions and the gags, making her laugh, but that advance took the bass out the beat and I became radio-friendly. What would I do if I was her? Probably what she's doing now.

The bus stops, I slide back down into a slouch position. A mother and her young son from the seat in front get up and get off, making me arch my neck to see. As they awkwardly shuffle down the aisle, her holding an umbrella in one hand whilst trying to maintain balance, she angrily tells him off about something and her aggy tone carries off down the stairs, like soapy bath water disappearing down a plug hole, and the bus moves off again. As I slowly lower my head back down, I notice that where the mum and son had just sat, there's a little finger-drawn dick and balls carefully crafted in the window's condensation, like a contribution to my very own Stations of the Cross. The little giggle that slips out my mouth is like a shot of sugar in a stewed cup of tea.

The big geezer's head is starting to lean towards me. I slip my hand in my pocket, pull out my phone and switch it off. Close my eyes again, thinking about breaded cod fillets, chips and beans.

THE ATHEIST

At a mate's birthday party, in this swanky bowling alley – yeah, swanky bowling alley, where the barmen did the top button up on their chequered shirts and wore five-panel caps acutely positioned on their heads, sleeves rolled up revealing fancy tattoos – a friend of a friend's boyfriend, who had a thick beard and a bobbly jumper, asked me if I was religious. I said:

'It depends what you mean, mate. I was raised a Catholic, my parents still practise,'

but before I could elaborate any further, he lunged two-footed into my conversational legs, launching into life like one of those shade-wearing sunflowers that danced upon a button being pressed, that for a while were a feature in many kids' bedrooms born in the eighties. He looked like he was born in the eighties, probably around my own age.

He leaned forward when he spoke, pretty sure he wagged a finger at one point too, stating how he hated it when Christians preached and that it was all scientifically flawed. He said Christians always refused to answer his questions on proof. Religion causes wars, he said, and has no place in modern society. And as for the Catholic Church, well, *you've* got a lot of answering to do. And he continued talking about paedophiles and embezzlement of funds and something about artefacts stashed in the Vatican.

I just looked at his bobbly jumper. Then at his beard. It was a good beard. Well looked after by the looks of things. He looked like the sort of dude that knew how to groom his beard. I assumed he applied some type of moisturising product, possibly conditioner? Were they the sort of product that advertised in men's magazines, with a glossy fold-out bit and a free sample? I wondered if he modelled his beard on a celebrity beard, like that geezer that used to play for Sheffield United, about twenty years ago. Alan Cork. Yeah, that was him, a vintage beard. Or was it more of a modern bearded sportsman? Like that forward at Man City. He's got a good beard too. The guy with the name that's spelt the same as Jesus, but pronounced differently. *That would be funny if it was him, wouldn't it?* I thought.

I looked around the room and there were a few beards in there that night, all of which seemed to be attached to bodies wearing bobbly jumpers and holding bottles of craft beer. His beard was the best, though, way better than mine. Mine was just stubble, with that weird bald bit to the right of my chin, like someone took a lawnmower to my face but just went in one straight line upwards from my jaw and couldn't be arsed with the rest.

I caught the end of his last sentence, something about that Dawkins guy, and when he finished, I said, 'Yeah, nice one, bruv,' and went and played pool with my mate Steve.

TRAP IT

I was walking home from work, tie and a shirt, trousers and shoes. Got to the green near my house; some young boys were kicking a football about. Full kit: replica tops, shirts, socks and astro boots. They must have been about ten. I must have been about thirty-three.

I was minding my own business, musing on the subtle difference between my favourite brands of crisps, Walkers Max and Real McCoy's, when one of the kids overhit a kick and that ball rolled over towards me.

I froze. Then my heartbeat rose, rapidly. Out of nowhere, I could suddenly hear a crowd, and my old football coach, all red-faced, bulging blood vessels in his neck, gruff cockney voice, West Ham tattoos and a pink Ralph, spit coming out of his mouth, screaming out at the top of his voice:

'PAUL! DON'T DO ANYTHING STUPID!
KEEP IT SIMPLE! KEEP IT SIMPLE!'

I took a breath, told myself:

Don't try and be flash,
just trap it,
get it under control and
just carefully
play it back.

Just before the ball reached my feet, another voice, deep inside the isolation unit of my mind, jumped up and screamed out:

PAUL! This is your chance,
you've gotta take it,
show them what you can do,
show them your skills!

Somewhere in between thinking about those two opposing views, I'd stuck my right leg out, and my right leg was confused, unsure what to do. The ball hit the outside of my black leather lace-up shoe, taking all the power out, and meekly trickled behind me, like water drops dribbling out of a tap in a drought, and rolled into the road, like my very own *You've Been Framed* video.

'Shit!'

I slapped my forehead. Just to rub salt into my wounds, I looked up, and the kids in the replica kits were laughing, and making wanker signs at me.

'You're rubbish, mate!'

I put my hands up.

'Sorry, boys, I
just ain't got it anymore.'

TWO TO TANGO

It takes two to tango,
it takes one to tread on the other's toes,
it takes two to build up the trust that the other is not gonna fuck it up again,
it takes one to fuck it up again,
it takes one to go.

ONE MORE

Round one, we arrive. Get a pint. Foster's, cooking lager.

'I wanna keep it light. Had a rough night last night, can't stay out too long.'

'What's wrong with you?' my mate says in jest, with an undertone that suggests, *You've changed. You left, I stayed. I'm hard, you're soft.*

'So be it,' I say. We plot down, while he gets the round in. Back home, Christmas Eve. Me, my mate and my brother, sat round a beer-stained table, windows sprayed snow-white in the corners. Old cockneys and Irish crowd the bar like punters at a car auction; the taller patrons brush their heads against the tacky paper chain decorations; it's warm. Don't recognise many faces, but the place hasn't changed.

Small talk begins, niceties are exchanged, 'Good to see you back here' and 'It's nice to be back,' I say, they say, and we skip through mortgages, kids, marriages, cars and careers, 'What you doing now, how's London?' Property prices, transport and crime appear in the conversation like constituents waiting at an MP's surgery, London provides the key and opinions rush the landlord.

Round two. 'Fosters is crap, innit?' I say, admitting my mistake. They laugh and I make that tactical upgrade to Kronenbourg, one that I've regretted in the past. Lug fast and it burns but it feels good.

Booze in the system, the Christmas season has seen me drinking like four nights in a row, hop-scotching from work dos and that, all shop talk, awkward exchanges and then to this, back home Christmas Eve, old mates, familiar place.

Smiles crack and we all begin to loosen. T's and th's start falling off, the first c-word gets dropped, as accents start slipping into them fitted cockney derivatives, treading paths parents and grandparents made to this place from London and beyond. 'Faack off' and 'Shaat up, mate,' we say, all sprayed with affection.

Round three. I see an old mate who I stand up to talk to. Five minutes into the chat and I get a tap on the arm, turn round and it's my brother and my mate and they're like, 'It's your round, son,' eyebrows up and down. I'm up to the bar and back again quick smart, a beer triangle in my hand, one I'm well practised in carrying. We sit down, we hear a bang and a few raised voices, door flies open and, on the pavement outside, we see two guys in each other's faces. We look out the window, pints in hand like we're sat in the grandstand at the races. Old Bill appear, they disappear, carted off in a meat wagon to the cages; a cheer goes up, it unites the pub and we laugh because *nothing changes.*

Round four and the talk is football and old computer games that we played, *Streets of Rage* and *Street Fighter II*, old holidays with mates and 'We should do this again,' we all say. But one by one we look at the time at ever-increasing intervals, something we never would've done. Until my mate finally breaks and says, 'I should probably go,' and I say, 'Yeah, I need to get back,' and my brother's like, 'Yeah, I gotta be up early,' and suddenly everything's changed.

It goes a bit quiet, as the last dregs get drunk and there's that slight pause before the exit. We're all thinking it. The Pogues come on the jukebox. At the bar I watch the landlord pour another pint and I turn round to the other two, shrug my shoulders, cheeky look on my face, and say, 'One more?'

BLAME IT ON THE TRACKING

I find rhymes in nothing,
take time to waste time
aged ten watching *Full Metal Jacket*,
aged thirty-three flying down the stairs on the mattress,
build affordable houses with matches,
slide down the property ladder and time it with some gadgets,
claim squatter's rights in the upper tax bracket,
facilitate conflict resolution workshops for gangsters,
lend money to bankers,
the whole thing's confused.

Must be your tracking, mate.

Take a Lynx can and a lighter, then blowtorch my bank account,
get low off the plastic fumes, then black out,
find happiness in sadness,
write an email, then fax it,
spell *backwards* backwards, then repackage it as forward,
take a rare bird song, then distort it,
add a beat and a verse, then record it,
repeat it ten times on an album,
release said album on MiniDisc,
the whole thing's confused.

Must be your tracking, mate.

Plan a world tour, then tour it,
book the parachute regiment to support it,
abort tour due to a bout of avian influenza,
spend time doing time in quarantine,
reflect on life via a Katie Price anthology,
lost boy on B wing,
boy found pronouncing Satan,
released on bad behaviour,
sign a book deal for six figs,
sell it exclusively at car-boots and primary school book weeks,
the whole thing's confused.

Must be your tracking, mate.

On the settee watching the telly whilst up in court as a witness.
Lilly, aged nine and a half, on behalf of the *Newsround* Press Pack,
ran an investigation into the business,
overpayment to a collection-evading Inland Revenue agent,
court fines agreed in monthly instalments of broken biscuits.
Retire to a tree in Fleet services,
junction 5 on the M3,
spend the kid's inheritance on a wild spree in the Wild Bean Café,
days spent watching reruns of Cup replays,
fixate on the buzz coming from the tape cassette,
playing DVDs on a VHS,
the whole thing's confused.

Must be your tracking, mate.

INFERNO

Stop. Just stop. Come out of there. Now. Come on. You can do it. Imagine your skin's a fireman's suit and you've just come out of a blazing inferno. And now you're condensation. We're gonna sack the body off for a bit, mate. Don't worry, it's cool, it'll still be there when you come back. Your head's way too hot right now and you're about to do some damage. We're just coming away for a bit, a'right? Nice.

You're out, yeah? Good. Now, look at the top of your head. Looks weird from this angle, don't it? Didn't realise your barnet was that dark? But still brown? Couple more greys now. There's your keyboard, by your body. It's a computer, mate. Just a computer. You were about to smash that up, you doughnut! That's the second time this week!

Right, slide up through them creaky floorboards. Imagine you're playing *Flashback* on the Mega Drive and you're the geezer slipping through the walls, on cheat mode. Keep rising, ignore your bedroom, it's a mess anyway. Up into the loft, with the light on, yeah. It's nice in here, it's that brown colour, what do they call it, sepia? You like that, don't you? Reminds you of that Santa's Christmas grotto they had at Collingwood Batchellor's, when you were a nipper.

Keep going up, through the chimney and onto the roof. Say 'alright' to the crows. Don't worry, they know what's going on, they know everything, you know that. Keep rising, mate, up into the clouds. It's a bit dark but you'll be alright, it's only a bit of rain, and besides, you like the rain; helps you to think, don't it? Watch out for the heron, he's on a mission, mate. You like seeing him fly; it's that wingspan, innit? Something else, mate.

Drop down a bit. Look, there's Cannon Hill Common. Looks sick up here, so much green, trees looking like broccoli stumps. That little dot pinging about on the grass is Ed, funny little dog, always sniffing trails, and there's the neighbours, casually strolling behind, they're always smiling.

Swing round, you can see right down Martin Way. The tops of the houses look cool up here, Morden's suburban uniform, looking like them little charity boxes we used to put money in at school, Cafod or whatever. Remember when Kevin knocked them off the cabinet in class and ended up pocketing loads of the coins, whilst getting praised for helping tidying up? Funny stuff. Wonder what he's up to now.

And there it is. The mighty Civic Centre, towering over the shops like a mother goose, with a load of little goslings in her breast. That's why it's curved, mate. It's like wings, but without wings, or arms, or any type of limb, but it don't matter; it's embracing the shops, protecting the town centre, letting that Crystal Palace phone tower in the distance know that we're no mugs here.

Swing left, there's that big derelict tower in Collier's Wood, looking like some mangled spring sticking out of a sofa. Mad, innit? Heard they're finally doing something with it. Probably flats, mate. Not for the likes of us, though, bruv.

How you feeling? Good? Drop back down now, careful as you descend. Imagine you're a magpie's feather falling from the sky on a cloudless day. Mind where you land, remember where you… no, you bellend, that's next door! Mind the washing. Lucky they're at the park, eh? Quick, jump the fence and through the back door, into the back room. Slip back inside the skin. Imagine you're on a really short water slide going in slow motion. Good?

Yeah, yeah, that's right, the kettle, stick it on, you know it makes sense. And for fuck's sake, Paul, don't make me do this again.

EPILOGUE:

Twenty Things I've Learnt from School and Work

1. Most of the stuff in that maths set you won't ever use, though, to be fair, the compass was pretty good for scratching Millwall graffiti into the exam desks.

2. There are eight eighths in an ounce and 3.4 grams in one eighth, though most people will mug you off and give you 2.5 grams, yet still call it an eighth.

3. On older car models, if you prise off the rubber from the passenger window with the use of a twisted coat hanger, you can open the door without a key.

4. On those cheap fluorescent cigarette lighters, you can wiggle the flame adjuster thing till it breaks, causing the lighter to become a mini-flamethrower every time you use it.

5. On those cheap fluorescent cigarette lighters, whilst on flamethrower mode, if you place a Polo in the flame it caramelises the sugar and gives it a whole new taste.

6. On those cheap fluorescent cigarette lighters, if you throw them really hard against the wall, they explode.

7. On those cheap fluorescent cigarette lighters, if you throw them really hard against the wall, and they explode, you might want to stand back; little bits break off and if they hit you it fucking hurts.

8. If you hold biros under the Bunsen burner flame you can mould them into some really interesting shapes, but those fumes give you a horrendous headache and are probably poisonous.

9. The way to spot a fake Ralph shirt is to look for the double stitching in the collar and if the ratio[1] between the horse and the jockey is just plain ridiculous.

---

1 *Ratio?* Shit, I did learn something after all!

10. Having the best trainers is not the be-all and end-all (though it is pretty sick. Not *that* sick, but still sick).

11. If people are giving you shit, and involving adults hasn't resolved the situation, approach them when they are all together in a group, find the biggest and hardest one and lamp the cunt. Observe how all the minions will peel away, like paint doused in thinner. Violence is rarely the answer, but standing up for yourself is something you should learn young. It's a lot harder to do later in life, when your self-confidence regularly takes a pathetic round-one exit from the Johnstone's Paint Trophy.

12. Throughout life, you'll probably have to get up early, probably five days a week, to go somewhere you probably don't want to go and do something you probably don't want to do and be ordered around by someone you probably don't like, just like school.

13. If there is something that you're interested in pursuing further, like, say, music or something, but someone says something like 'most people don't make it' or 'there's no money in that,' ignore them and just do it. There's hardly any money in anything anyway, unless you went to one of them private schools.

14. There are some things that you'll just have to learn yourself if you want to understand them, like finding out what left-wing and right-wing means, and that money you get given from credit cards and loans isn't yours, you have to pay it back because of this thing called APR, and if you don't, you get those red letters and those bastards phone you, a lot, and they keep phoning you until you pay (and telling them to fuck off does you no favours).

15. Unless you get a trade, join the army, get really lucky or do A-levels and get a degree, or by default are swimming in privilege, there aren't a lot of options for you, and you may well end up in one of those jobs where you're sat in a call centre and you have to phone people who haven't paid

back their credit card or loan, a lot, and you have to keep phoning them until they pay (even if they tell you to fuck off, which they will).

16. The best thing you could and should have learned at school is learning how to learn. Regardless of what you're studying, whether it's trigonometry or simply trying to assemble IKEA flatpack furniture, the skill of applying yourself to something never ever changes. Learning that skill later in life is really fucking hard and pretty embarrassing when you realise most other people have been doing it for years and you were too busy dicking about or daydreaming, thinking about girls you'd never ask out, or shelling it down on the mic at a huge illegal outdoor rave, the type of which doesn't exist anymore.

17. Despite all of the above, even if you didn't do very well at school, or you suck at your job, it doesn't mean you've failed. Life can take some interesting twists and new roads present themselves all the time if you look hard enough. (Just don't take those new roads as an excuse to park the car up and get caned with your mates. It's a good laugh, but it really slows you down and you'll end up doing something a bit crap with your life, like writing poems or watching shit YouTube videos about chemtrails, where they're far too reliant on the eerie one-note synthesiser sound.)

18. Writing poems and stories isn't necessarily for bellends or people that get high marks at school and have good spelling.

19. Dinner parties and dating are actual things and don't just exist on bland American sitcoms.

20. Writing poems and stories isn't crap; it can be a lot of fun. Same goes for performing. There is definitely something to be said for doing something just for the sake of doing it. You can have many wonderful experiences doing this and there's probably worse ways to live your life.